THE WOMEN WERE LEAVING THE MEN

THE WOMEN WERE LEAVING THE MEN

Stories by
Andy Mozina

Wayne State University Press   Detroit

© 2007 by Wayne State University Press,
Detroit, Michigan 48201.

Manufactured in the
United States of America.

11 10 09 08 07   5 4 3 2 1

Library of Congress Cataloging-in-Publication Data

Mozina, Andrew, 1963–
The women were leaving the men / Andy Mozina.
p. cm. — (Made in Michigan writers series)
ISBN-13: 978-0-8143-3362-4 (pbk. : alk. paper)
ISBN-10: 0-8143-3362-1 (pbk. : alk. paper)
1. Intimacy (Psychology)–Fiction. I. Title.
PS3613.O96W66 2007
813'.6–dc22
2007005250

 michigan council for
arts and cultural affairs

This book is supported by the Michigan
Council for Arts and Cultural Affairs.

∞ The paper used in this publication meets
the minimum requirements of the
American National Standard for
Information Sciences—Permanence of
Paper for Printed Library Materials, ANSI
Z39.48-1984.

Book design by Lisa Tremaine
Typeset by Maya Rhodes
Composed in Meta and Proforma

For Madeleine: young person, young reader

CONTENTS

Acknowledgments ix

Cowboy Pile 1

Privacy, Love, Loneliness 7

The Enormous Hand 22

My Way of Crying 51

Beach 76

The Arch 81

Moon Man 103

The Love Letter 119

The Women Were Leaving the Men 136

The Housekeeper's Confession 147

My First Cake Was a Failure 167

Lighter Than Air 177

Admit 202

ACKNOWLEDGMENTS

THANKS TO MY earliest writing teachers who sent me down the trail: Arthur Morey, Sheila Schwartz, and Leslie Epstein. Thanks to all who read various drafts of these stories, especially Bonnie Jo Campbell, Lisa Lenzo, Mike Stefaniak, Julia Hanna, Mary Winifred Hood, and Jeff Schwaner, with an extra cold Pabst Blue Ribbon raised to Mark Wisniewski, adroit editor and indispensable coach. I'm also indebted to M. W. Hood and J. Schwaner for publishing some of my earliest efforts in *Captain Kidd Monthly.* Thanks to Byrd Leavell for his above-and-beyond efforts on behalf of this manuscript. Thanks to my father for giving me the books without which this book wouldn't exist, and thanks to my mother for her support. Thanks to my wife, Lorri, also without whom these stories didn't and wouldn't exist. I'm also grateful for the generosity of Kalamazoo College, especially support received through the Marlene Crandell Francis Trustee Professorship.

People ought to know that the hair shirt scene in "The Housekeeper's Confession" takes off from a somewhat similar scene in J. F. Powers's novel *Wheat That Springeth Green,* a book to which I am indebted for certain factual aspects of priestly life in the sixties and seventies.

It should also be noted that while "Moon Man" is based upon some details surrounding the *Apollo 16* mission, my story and characters are entirely fictional. The actual *Apollo 16* mission was launched April 16, 1972, and included crew members Captain John W. Young, commander; Lieutenant Commander Thomas K. Mattingly II, Command Module pilot; and Lieutenant Colonel Charles M. Duke Jr., Lunar Module pilot.

I gratefully acknowledge the magazines in which these stories have appeared, usually in slightly different form: "Cowboy Pile," *Beloit Fiction Journal;* "Privacy, Love, Loneliness," originally published as "Ten-Inch Tommy," *West Branch;* "The Enormous Hand," *Beloit Fiction Journal;* "My Way of Crying," originally published as "We Love Each Otter," *The Florida Review;* "Beach," *The Massachusetts Review;* "The Arch," *The Massachusetts Review;* "Moon Man," *Alaska Quarterly Review;* "The Love Letter," *Fence;* "The Women Were Leaving the Men," *Tin House;* "The Housekeeper's Confession," *Third Coast;* "My First Cake Was a Failure," originally published as "Effigy," *Rambunctious Review;* "Lighter Than Air," *Maisonneuve.*

Cowboy Pile

Out on the ranges, out West, you get cowboy piles. Mounds of human cowboys. A cowboy lies on the ground (for no reason, it seems), and then somebody lies across him, and then a third guy piles on. Then one after another. Sometimes you'll see a pile from the Interstate. If the wind's right and your window is down and your engine's running gently, you might hear six guns fired into the air or the barely audible hooting and yowling of a convocation of cowboys. If you're lucky, ahead of you on the highway you'll see a pickup with a pair of men wearing ten-gallon hats. Follow those gents. Exit.

With about twenty or thirty guys, the cowboy pile is at a turning point. By now the cowboys on the bottom are suffocating, dying. They may wonder why they're in a pile and not rounding up wild horses, or punching dogies, or branding calves. Many pilers, no doubt, are thinking immortality or at least a flash of glory: more than most people, cowboys are subject to the lure of legend. After a memorable cowboy pile, it's the guys who started it that get sung around the fire, and if sustaining a collapsed rib cage or even dying is a way of proving you were on the bottom—well, so be it. A few have grown up in cities; they've done phone booths, Volkswagens: they're known as "seeds." They're a little older. Tend to be suffering under various intellectual and spiritual exasperations. The rest are young guys usually. Guys with maybe some spurs to earn. Guys with maybe no spurs to lose.

(Have cowboy piles been treated in the legal arena? Once, a pile set off a "wrongful death action." Guy on the bottom had left a note on his kitchen table saying his foreman had mentally harassed him and driven him to suicide. Cowboy pile was the best way to go, he figured. Lawyers for the cowboy's estate argued that "the suicide directly resulted from the foreman's intentional infliction of emotional distress." The judge, however, said that "suicide constitutes a break in the causal chain," that it is never "reasonably foreseeable under the circumstances," and so the harassment could not be the "proximate cause" of the suicide. [See *The Estate of Chet Edwards v. Stanley Meat Consortium,* (1989) 79 Tex.3d 179, 182 27 S.W.2d 793, 796.] In the end, strange to say, the cowboy pile itself was not an issue in the case.)

The great saguaro cactus can grow ten men high. A great cowboy pile can grow as many men high as men can stand men. The turning point is mainly a battle between exhilaration and qualms. Exhilaration that the pile is significant with the potential for being a whopper. Qualms due to screams of pain, bones breaking, cowboys weeping, regrets. You know: "Get the hell off me!" Or: "I can't breathe!"

It ain't a cartoon, somebody on top thinks. *We're for real.* Then he makes a choice. Does he give in to reality or does he go for legend? He's on top of the pile, riding tall, so to speak. He stands to gain, it would seem, if the pile keeps piling. More than your average folk, cowboys are subject to the lure of lore, the love of legend. The guy may stay on and a guy on the brink of death may die, and so his wailing stops. Maybe two wailers die. If the remaining cowboys are reckless enough, they'll willfully interpret the end of the wailing as an end of the pain; therefore, no need to depile. (This apparently irrational phenomenon is now under study by experts in paranormal perception, mob dynamics, religious ritual. Writing in *Omni*, Benjamin Halsted, a sociologist from the University of Wisconsin, calls it "a headlong rush to annihilation, driven by the pleasure of loss of self in community, accompanied by an intense realization of our collective oneness, a sense of The All-In-All. Paradoxically, this need for oneness is showing up so acutely among a class of individuals widely known for their independence of spirit.") And so the qualms level drops and the exhilaration level crosses the line into frenzy.

Eyewitness News may be on hand by this time, the reporter like a sanctimonious hockey announcer when a fight breaks out on the ice. (Seven percent of cowboys are former adult amateur or professional hockey players.) The reporter's righteousness may, of course, spark some spite among the snakeskin-boot crowd within the viewing area. They may head for the cowboy pile to show Wade "Son-of-a-Bitch" Barley, Eyewitness News, just what he can do with his lack of respect for legend and lore. So say it swells. Forty, fifty guys.

Just as talk of a record pile gets going, the police drag themselves in. Though it surprises almost everybody, the one interprofessional brotherhood in the world that really matters is the one between policemen and cowboys. (Thirteen percent of all cowboys have attended at least two weeks in an accredited police academy.) And cops protect their own—even if it means letting them kill themselves. For every cowpoke they pull off, they let two, three, four pile on. Some cops pretend to help untangle the mess but "accidentally" fall on the pile themselves. Cops respect legend, lore.

Ribs crackle like a hearty campfire.

Somebody'll take a picture for a postcard: Huge jackalope, complete with rider, hopping over a cowboy pile. Sterno, Wyoming, Cowboy Pile Capital of the Free World, etc.

Experienced pilers will often make an effort to let somebody near death crawl out. Through brute strength (some who've been delivered in this way say "supernatural force"), a bubble of relaxed pressure rises around the beleaguered piler. This individual "rides the bubble" to safety. Or maybe not. If you make it out, you're supposed to pile on. Cowboy code. Most guys do, but not before a pinch of Copenhagen, a few hits of oxygen, and a quick interview with Eyewitness News.

"How's the pile?"

"Harsh. Real compacted."

"Who started it?"

"Guy named Tad. He's from outta town. That's his guitar case."

"Is he a cowboy?"

"He said he was."

"How many have to die before this crazy fad runs its course?"

"I'd say about sixteen in one pile. That would ruin it for me." He spits, breaks a tobacco-stained smile. "No, seriously, no one wants anyone to get hurt."

"But in a pile this size?"

"Well, Mister, you may be right, you may be wrong, but it's my duty to pile on."

He does. A Dodge Dart pulls up in a cloud of dust. Out staggers an eighty-nine-year-old man. Identifies himself as a happy but finished individual. Says he always wanted to die crushed in a cowboy pile. He doesn't stay for too many questions. He circles the pile, calling for an entry bubble. It takes ten minutes but somebody gets spit out, unconscious, maybe dead; paramedics carry him from the scene. (Paramedics have gone back and forth on the issue, picketing and then letting be, at times trying to break a pile but more often merely "servicing" it. "You can't help people won't help themselves," they say.) Before the bubble closes, the old man crawls in, content, briefly famous in life, likely to be sung in death. He's dressed for the occasion: Stetson, starched white shirt, oil-black boots. If he has any sense for lore, the pockets of his Levi's are stuffed with handfuls of white sagebrush flowers.

Panic may set in before the pile gets too compacted. This can lead to what is called a "flapjack," where the pile spreads and flattens like batter on a griddle. The flattening occurs as men try to get away from one another's elbows, flails, kicks, twists, writhings. A sort of centrifugal force develops. There are displays of superhuman strength. Many new injuries occur. Often a flapjack is more interesting to watch than a tall but relatively calm pile. Sometimes depiling is achieved without death, though almost never without serious injury. The look on the men's faces as they come to their senses is awe, relief, anger. Some consult the sky. Many knock their hats back into shape on their chaps, then put those hats on their heads. A spooked, trembling cowboy lights a crushed cigarette. A lanky buckaroo says, "Sheee-it!" You won't hear a whole lot else. And whatever brought these men together rises into the air like smoke, and each man will question whether what was had to be and whether what wasn't should have been.

Sometimes, though, when the pile has reached a certain magnitude, a muffled, ragged song begins to percolate up through the cowboys. It's generally a song about a lonesome range, a hell of a horse, a brave brand inspector, brucellosis, coyotes, an inexplicable stampede, a woman left behind somewhere like a favorite rope and then lost. The song usually begins deep in the pile—some say from the mouths of crushed cowboys already called to the last roundup. The tune spreads gradually, like a flame through kindling, until it gathers force, tempo, a harmony rooted in the deep-bottomed sound of a pile of men. New cowboys practically tiptoe onto the pile, like parishioners late for mass, but they do keep piling. A scrappy tenor might stand on the pile's peak, holding his hat over his ram's-horn belt buckle with two hands. He takes a solo. The trail is rued, the trail is praised. His voice rides wind and is gone. Then, all together, the cowboys take the refrain. They sing legends, they sing lore; they sing themselves to death.

Stand pileside and listen. Listen to the cowboys sing.

Privacy, Love, Loneliness

I saw Gracie by my locker after school, tall and thin like bamboo, in her earth-tone blouse and skirt, and that really set me off. I wanted to tackle her, just for fun, and lie on top of her, maybe wrestle. I wanted to be up against her—not mean. I was vibrating like something out of whack. I came closer and she said, "Hi," and I said, "You're standing by my locker."

She smiled. We had talked before. In chemistry class. That was fun. Now, though, it was too much. The way she was smiling. "Do you mind if I get something out of my locker?" I said, dropping my book bag.

"Sure," she said, and she stepped aside.

When I didn't care, I had a way of talking that she liked, but now I cared, so I couldn't talk. I took my English notebook out of my locker and held it with two hands, like a fancy plate. "Can I talk to you later?" I said, walking away. "Please, don't try to follow me."

"Hey, I wanted to talk to you."

"I'm not safe to be around right now."

"You're telling me," she yelled, and she stomped the heel of her right foot, still standing by my locker. I was robbing us of something important; I was acting like a criminal with the materials of daily life.

Leaving her, I had a charge of energy in me. I felt like a Gumby action figure with his wire skeleton, and the charge was making my inner wire hum. I took this feeling and pushed it and felt very fucked up in the head. My father had left when I was four, and this was always a good excuse for fucked-up behavior.

When I got home from school, I felt slimy and sweaty and hungry. I made a peanut butter sandwich, and eating that sandwich made me feel even greasier. The doorbell rang, but I ignored it. I was the only one home, and my ma wouldn't be back from work for maybe two hours. The bell rang again. This extra ring changed my feeling about answering the door.

I stole a quick look out the little window in the front door. Gracie had just moved away from the door, so she didn't see me see her. When she stepped off the porch, she was carrying two book bags. One of them was mine. I ducked into the living room and watched her out the picture window, walking across the front lawn, heading for the side yard. I scooted down the hall into the bathroom, to the open window, and looked between the curtains: she went through the side yard, her feet swishing the thick grass. The back doorbell rang, and I laughed hysterically, which was very dumb, because I'm sure she could hear me outside. I went into the kitchen and sat under the table. Thinking about her bambooness made me crazy to see her; I didn't even care about the emotional dangers that can happen when two people try to know each other. I just wanted to see her and be with her. Being alone so much was making me more crazy. Sometimes I was okay talking to certain kids at school, but I never really made friends with them outside of school, except Bill Hampton, but he turned into a drug addict. Gracie would be a good friend in the world. But not yet. Not this instant.

I waited until she was gone. Then I checked the back porch and found my book bag wedged between the big door and the screen door. When I touched the bag, I almost burst into flames. Remembering how slimy and greasy and smelly I was, I took a shower and masturbated about Gracie. Then I wanted to get dressed faster than I had ever gotten dressed before—I pulled on one of my good old socks too quickly and put my toes right through it.

Death of a sock, I thought. The whole situation was fucked up in a way I was very fond of at the time. It really plucked my wire. I heated a jar of spaghetti sauce for dinner, spilled orange juice on my pants, argued with the television, pushed the toaster off the counter, and ran about six inches of cool water into the sink. I went back to my room, where I had left the dead sock on the floor. I carried the sock into the living room and pushed some furniture around to give it space. I knew that this behavior would not go over well with other people and that if I wanted to know Gracie I would have to change my ways. But first I would have a ritual burial.

I gathered some of my still-good socks and put them around the dead sock. Then, in a circle around this, I arranged other household stuff that resembled the sock: a rubber glove, the sheath for an umbrella, mittens, shoes. In the next orbit I stuck less-related items: an inner tube, a rolled-up poster of Kareem Abdul-Jabbar, a T-shirt. Then, the television, the blender, a fifty-cent piece. In the last circle, I put a tiny pyramid of aluminum foil. I looked at this careful funeral and told myself that from now on I would be more normal. Then I put the book bag that Gracie had touched on top of the dead sock. I stepped back. The old order no longer made sense now that the thing Gracie had touched was in the center. This would be my new motto: let the thing that Gracie touches be at the center. This would organize everything else. Just thinking about my motto made the world warm and sweet.

I was just putting the TV back when Ma came home, wearing a curly wig and a white outfit with a fancy-looking digital watch hanging from her neck. She was a nurse's aide in a locked ward at Sunnyvale Nursing Home.

"How were they today?" I asked.

"They've all got a lot on their minds," she said, dog-tired, but half-smiling to herself. She took a can of diet root beer from the fridge, told me to give her a half hour before putting dinner on the table, went into her room, and closed the door.

If she'd seen the sock funeral, I could have told her it was a science project—make your own solar system—or I could have told her something more true. She'd had her own tough times and knew that trying to be happy was complicated.

After dinner my new personality dragged me to the phone and made me call Gracie. I apologized for being a jerk, thanked her for returning my book bag, and asked her to sit next to me at the movies. Gracie suggested instead that we go to Ten-Inch Tommy's, where she thought we could get served beer. I wanted Gracie to like me, so I said, "Sure."

We tooled out there in my ma's 1978 LTD. It was a date. Tommy's bar was a tall A-frame buried in the woods, a half hour outside Wausau. The walls were covered with business cards, a pair of stuffed bobcats, a few deer heads. Tommy nodded to Gracie when we walked in, but he looked like he might never smile. He had a crew cut and a big bristly Popeye jaw; you could tell he looked older than his age. We took a wobbly table along the wall opposite the

bar and Gracie got us a pair of tap beers. The place was pretty quiet.
The overhead TV was on, but the sound was way down. Three guys
were at the bar, and I thought that they and Tommy were going to
listen to our conversation, but then they must have gotten over our
interruption and went back to talking, something about Tommy's
cirrhosis of the liver and stupid doctors.

Since I had picked up Gracie I hadn't said very much to her.
Driving out to Tommy's, I probably paid too much attention to the
power windows, trying to create a certain cool cross-breeze that I'd
become convinced was essential to the moment. I had heard that
you should "be yourself" on dates. I was definitely being myself,
which was all inward and fucked up. But I really wanted to be my
new, more friendly self. Except it was hard to change. So we hadn't
talked. I had no idea who she was, though at the time, honestly, it
wasn't a big issue with me. I think my silence was getting on her
nerves, though, because when she sat down after getting the beers,
she said "so" in that leading way. She swept her hair back over her
head and raised her eyes to me. Her face was almost perfectly dia-
mond-shaped. She had big cheekbones and a weak chin.

"My God, you know your face is really great." I laughed because I
saw how she must have seen me saying that.

"Just relax, Brian." Her voice was a little bit husky. "It's nice of
you, but you don't have to compliment my looks. I'm not going to
compliment yours."

"Oh, you shouldn't."

"Yeah, anyway, I just thought you might like Tommy's. It's quiet,
we can talk."

"Is that a big thing with you?"

"What? Talking? I don't know if it's a *big* thing. It's a thing I
like."

"I like to drink," I said.

"You do? You say that in kind of a weird way. Like you're making fun of me."

"Oh no, I'm not." Then I thought for a second. "You can tell how my voice is?"

She did a double take. I sensed things were not going well. "Listen, are you all right?"

"Yeah, sure. I mean, I definitely am."

"Well, then just relax, okay?"

"Yeah, I want to. Thanks for saying that."

She frowned a little, then said, "I'm getting some chips."

I watched her body as she went toward the bar, rubbing her arms like she was keeping mosquitoes off. I wanted her face and body in a very controlled way. This became clear to me. I wanted to have her with me inside my head just as if she were me: there would be no separation. I had no idea what this would mean for her. I was already thinking about masturbating with these memories when I got home, when I could have the experience without the tension of being so *with* her. The excitement was making me crazy. Luckily I remembered my pledge to be a normal person with her. I thought it would be very normal to ask her about herself. She came back and gave me a bag of Sergeant Morris potato chips. I'd never heard of that brand. They were made in Morris, Wisconsin.

"Tell me about yourself," I said, squeezing the bag open with a pop.

Although I did want to know, she laughed. Then I laughed, too. When we both laughed, I felt we were close in a way that was easier to take. That was how it had been in chemistry class. From that point on, I tried to get her to laugh with me if I could. But this time she didn't laugh for long. She said, "Do you really want to know?"

"Yeah, definitely. Trust me. I don't know. I'm just saying things. Trust me."

"I'll try," she said. Then she told me she hoped she was one of those people who blossomed after high school, because things now were mainly a drag. She couldn't believe what most people thought was cool; she was disgusted by the guys she had dated. She told me about her parents and how they were basically okay, except they expected a lot from her and her dad worked too much as a big honcho at the paper company and her mom told her too much private stuff, like about her sex life. But she didn't hate them or anything. She wanted to be a fashion designer. Then I was supposed to talk.

I told her that I was pretty good at being in the world. Reality for me was like falling off a log. She laughed but asked me if I was playing mind games with her. I told her that if I was, I didn't mean to at all. She told me people who played mind games were usually trying to get some sort of power over someone else. I said this was interesting. Then I put two and two together and said I was not trying to get power over her. She smiled to herself and then asked what my folks were like.

I told her my mom was cool but sort of sad and that my dad had disappeared when I was four. She seemed to like the fact that my dad had done this; she became more interested in me, so I told her more. I remembered two things about my dad: that he had a bushy beard and that he played golf. He used to practice hitting chip shots to little holes he'd carved out of our lawn. When I was older I caddied at the country club and watched golf on TV, and I noticed that golfers almost never had beards—and nothing close to the bushy one my dad had. I explained to Gracie how this had led me to ask strangers, people from out of town or kids coming back from vacations, if they'd seen any bearded golfers. I didn't tell people why I was asking, so they just thought I was crazy. Gracie said that what I did didn't sound crazy to her.

I thought this would relax me, but it didn't. I felt extremely tense for about thirty seconds. What I didn't tell her was that I thought my dad must be an unusual person to be a bearded golfer and that I saw this as another excuse to be fucked up, having his unusual genes, etc. To change the subject, I said that I thought books were very cool, and she agreed and said she didn't mean not to trust me at first. I told her I thought she was great and beautiful. She got a little embarrassed but said she thought I was all right. I wanted to get away from her and masturbate so badly I was going to explode. When I finally took her home, she patted the seat between us before she got out of the car and said we should get together again.

This was a shock for me. I became happy.

So then for a while I was happy because she accepted me; I must have looked fairly normal to her. Or maybe she was desperate. She was always telling me about these assholes she used to date, guys who were too aggressive or too stupid or too selfish or something.

We didn't go to the movies very often; Ten-Inch Tommy's became our place. After a while, Tommy even nodded at me when I came in. He told me he was only ten inches tall, which I found out was his way of accepting you into his gang. He winked at me when he told me this, like I'd know exactly what he meant, but I didn't wink back. I didn't want anything extra to do with him. Sometimes his rants to his cronies were a little unsettling. I overheard him telling them that logging was shaving the earth's head, and about how he wasn't born of the Virgin Mary nor was he Lucifer's busboy but he was set into the fabric of the world as a kind of universal joint and linchpin. One time he said "Pecker!" really loud when I was putting our glasses on the bar on our way out. I asked Gracie about that, and she said Tommy was just a drunk, basically, and when he was drunk there was no point listening to him. But I didn't know how to tell her that grizzled, drunk old men yelling "pecker" in my direction scared me, and I didn't know how to ask her if she knew that sometimes Tommy looked at her like he wanted to completely understand her bambooness.

* * *

At the Fourth of July fireworks, Gracie and I held hands almost through the entire show. When it was over, I told Gracie in her ear that I loved her a lot, tons and tons, though I'm not sure what I meant by this. People were walking by our blanket with their coolers and their folded lawn chairs and their neon snakes. She didn't say she loved me. She said she "liked" me. She said she liked me because I was "different." This seemed to mean my normalcy campaign was failing, but I knew that people like Gracie went for a normal sort of differentness. It was the deranged way of being different that I was afraid she would see in me. As far as our "relationship" went, she said we shouldn't go overboard. I told her I was very onboard. But for a while I stopped saying I loved her. I thought I would lie low for a while when it came to love.

Then one night, after we'd been to Tommy's, she told me to drive over near the quarry and park the car. I knew that it was time for sex. She smiled at me and climbed into the backseat.

"Come on back, the water's fine," she said. Which I knew to be a joke.

"I'm coming," I said, very innocently.

"Give me a break!"

We started kissing, and the telltale undressing was going on. This was obvious to me. It was also obvious to me that I needed a working erection or I was going to be in big trouble. But the actual existence of Gracie next to me was still very problematic.

So I said, "Hello, my name is Mark, what's yours?"

"My name is Gracie, what's yours?" she answered, confused.

"My name is Betty, what's yours?"

She looked almost in shock. I pleaded with my eyes until she said, "Um, my name is Sandy, what's yours?"

I will always owe Gracie for that moment when she took a chance and didn't let me twist in the wind without a usable identity. We exchanged names and personalities until we finally made love with me as Johnny, a bisexual construction worker (I didn't tell her I was bisexual), and Gracie as Ginnie, a young accountant.

In the middle of things, she was very energetic. I decided she wasn't faking. Then I enjoyed it and, as soon as I enjoyed it, it was over.

When we uncoupled, I swear to God the car was levitating and rotating slowly like one of those restaurants on top of a huge building. I felt extremely giddy and giggled like a defective. But I realized that it was probably strange to giggle after sex. I was ruining it, and this made the giggling snowball uncomfortably.

This was not just "different" but "nuts." I took off the rubber and tied the open end in a knot and placed it on the floor of the car, thinking I'd keep it in my junk drawer as a souvenir—and this set me off giggling again.

"Please, Brian. Easy." There was some pleading in her voice, more anxiety than I'd ever heard from her. Calming me down and calming herself down seemed like the same thing, and I saw some of the effect I was having on her, saw a little bit of her emotional life, and that got to me.

We maneuvered so we could get both our arms around each other and we hugged really hard. I settled down. We hugged each other. It was very sincere. It was probably the greatest moment so far in my life. I said, "I love you, Gracie." I was *very* happy. She hugged me more but just said, "Oh, Brian." With the deed done, I had forgotten that I had to pretend to be someone else to do it.

Then we dawdled in the backseat. We got silly and started playing that game—rock, scissors, paper. Rock breaks scissors, scissors cuts paper, paper covers rock. I told her that I liked what this game said about things, namely, that all power was relative. She said she had never thought about it like that but it seemed true enough. After a while I suggested we play a variation: privacy, love, loneliness. Privacy excludes love, love beats loneliness, loneliness pries open privacy, since if you got too lonely you'd be willing to give up some of your privacy. Privacy was a fist, loneliness was one finger, love was two fingers. Gracie gave me a sad, dreamy, emotional look but said, "Why not?"

So we played privacy, love, loneliness in the backseat of my mother's 1978 LTD. Then we fell asleep for about an hour under a blanket and woke up with strange patterns from the seat on our bodies.

The next time we went to Tommy's, I knew we would probably end up at the quarry again. I was a little embarrassed that we had had to make up personalities so I could have sex. My whole normalcy campaign was really hurt by that performance. I was sure

Gracie had a little speech prepared for the backseat about how I should calm down and trust her and stop pulling stunts. And I thought this was directly related to why she wouldn't say she loved me. I thought for sure she would have said it after we had sex. Between those two dates, I got maybe an hour of loopy, hallucinating sleep each night, because I was always thinking about whether she loved me and what would happen if she wouldn't let me be someone else if we had sex again.

When we walked into Ten-Inch Tommy's that night, I must have had a pretty miserable look on my face because as soon as the screen door wheezed shut behind us, Tommy shouted from his stool behind the bar, "Well, look what the cat dragged in!"

This time I did wink at Tommy just to show him no hard feelings, we were square, in the same gang. Rough jokes were okay, but no hostility.

"You seen a ghost?" Tommy shouted, turned from me. He wore a white T-shirt and was rubbing a speck of something on the counter. Three of his cronies roosted along the bar. One of them gave me an eye.

"Tommy's got a bee in his bonnet," I said quietly to Gracie, hoping that would be the end of it. We both sat at our wobbly table instead of me getting the first round, like I'd been doing.

"What's up?" she said.

"Let him settle down a little."

"Do you want me to get it?"

"No, I'll do it. Just not right now."

"He doesn't mean anything," she said.

"Yeah, definitely," I said.

She watched me. I tried not to show that I was starting to vibrate like something out of whack. But I felt like telling her that she wanted a contradiction, that she wanted everything to be different plus okay and normal.

Tommy had been mumbling something, and then his voice went louder: "I ain't your pa, your God-the-Father, and I ain't got the money for groceries—you bet yer ass. This ain't the free world. This ain't rock 'n' roll."

"Then what is it?" a crony asked.

"It's what's up here, in your noggin: crucified, died, and was buried. Arose in his head."

"Jeez Louise, this is ridiculous," I said in a hollow voice. I felt sweat break out above my hairline.

"Do you want me to . . . ?" Gracie asked. Her voice covered up something Tommy was saying. But then I heard him.

"There's a history of it!" Tommy announced. "In the family!"

There was an uproar from the cronies, disputing or agreeing I couldn't tell.

"I need to not be here," I said.

"My folks are out," she said, almost shy, on her own train of thought, as if she were completely untouched by Tommy, and the home we were going to was exactly why she could be so untouched.

"That's great," I said, though a fear of making love to her shivered through me. Then I leaned across the table, before the sweat could start running down my face, and whispered into her ear, "I want to make love to you so bad."

I sat back and Gracie looked at me, dreamy and intense and serious, but then she smiled, like something crucial had been settled, and we got up. I took her hand and led us out of there, but I felt like it was the other way around, that I was a balloon floating behind her on a string. As we were leaving, I heard Tommy yell, "Because I say so!"

We drove to Gracie's house. I powered down all the windows and a tremendous refreshing wind swept through the car and whipped some of her hair and levitated the rest in gentle, magical-looking curves, and I calmed down a lot. Gracie reached over and took my right hand and said, "You're all right. I really like you." Her tone was encouraging and pleased, and I traced it to what I had whispered in her ear. Either she was ignoring that I'd been skittish at Tommy's, or I was just getting good at appearing normal.

She lived in a big modern house by the river. I automatically took my shoes off when we got inside, and so did Gracie: it was that kind of place. For some reason, she didn't turn on any lights as we went through the house and up the wide, carpeted staircase to the third level. Because we were quiet, I knew what was about to happen. I wasn't at all ready for it, but apparently at Tommy's I had managed to sound ready. The house was air-conditioned and I shivered. At the top of the stairs, Gracie took a right into a room and flicked on the light. It was a bathroom and she closed the door. I stood by myself in the dark hallway. The carpet was so thick I couldn't see the light under the bathroom door. There was a skylight at the end of the hall. I walked down there, the sound of her putting down the toilet seat fading behind me. Moonlight was coming in. A plush chair sat under the skylight, next to a lamp and a little bookcase. I took down my pants and underwear, feeling my cold hands against my legs. I sprawled in the moonlight and worked on getting an erection. My hands were downright icy, nothing seemed to work. I couldn't actually see the moon from where I was sitting, but I needed to see it. I stood on the chair and there it was. A bright dime.

I heard the toilet flush. The sound of it, muffled, at this distance, really got to me, reminded me of distant family times, of times at home. I was in a different house now. It felt like being inside a giant head, but not exactly the head I'd grown up in, and Gracie was there with me, where I had always wanted her, but nothing felt right. I had the weird sense that Tommy had followed us, that he had known Gracie for a long time, that he might step out from behind one of the doors I passed in the hallway and stand between us. Then the door opened and she came out. Just before she turned off the bathroom light, I could see she was wearing only a bra and panties.

She looked right where I was. I stood on the chair, in moonlight, with my pants down. I had told her that I wanted to make love to her and now I knew that I couldn't try to do it as someone else. She walked toward me, the tallest and thinnest bamboo. If I could have known that things were going to work out, that my mind or my body wouldn't give me away, it would have been the greatest thing imaginable to see her coming toward me like that. I could see how there might be bliss in the world, if certain things were for sure.

The Enormous Hand

The enormous hand was in fact a natural part of Bill's human body and, for daily household cleaning, was fitted with sponges and veined with tubes that dispensed solvents and cleansers and deodorizers. The heavy-handedness of Bill drew taunts, which he sometimes answered with crushing retaliations and vindictive grippings, but whenever there was a jelly spill or a piece of gum stepped on, Bill moved his enormous hand into action. He could clean and rinse messes instantly. To supply the hand with the liquids it needed to perform its function, Bill wore a Cleaning Agent Dispenser Backpack, which he decorated with anti-dirt slogans in black Magic Marker—"Mighty Tidy!" "Wash = Love" "Wipe It Down!"—and onto which he skillfully decoupaged the wrapper from a package of Brawny paper towels, adopting the thick-haired, vaguely bucktoothed lumberjack as his emblem of overwhelming cleaning power.

Bill became well known for the cleaning abilities at his fingertips. He got a call from a local TV station doing a series on handicapped and/or grotesquely deformed people who nevertheless weren't mopes or drains on society but rather "took the *dis-* out of *disability*" and led productive lives and inspired everyone, and so Bill was interviewed on TV. Thus did the public witness the hydraulic wizardry of Bill's Cleaning Agent Dispenser System, and thus did the public learn that Bill's enormous hand, which was his right hand, measured, when splayed, approximately twenty-four inches from the tip of his pinkie to the tip of his thumb, and that when this hand was stripped of its gadgetry and immersed in a tub of water, it displaced exactly one cubic foot of water. It was the biggest hand anyone had ever seen.

The interviewer made all kinds of jokes, like "Let me shake your hand," and when the interview was over he invited every viewer to "give Bill a hand." Bill took this so-called joking the wrong way and said "Fuck you!" to the TV guy. It's possible that Bill's swear words were so shocking that they burst through the TV station's swear filters or leapt across the live feed's six-second delay, or maybe the censor was asleep at the switch (and in fact, allegations of nonfeasance and conspiracy to commit obscenity were filed against her)— in any case, those exact dirty words were broadcast on *Live at Five News*, along with the visual of Bill's enormous palm advancing to blot out the camera's view, a gesture that darkened screens in such an absolute and disconcerting way that more than a few viewers felt themselves entering the bottomless black bag of death itself.

Many viewers, as well as many informed nonviewers, were offended at this use of an obscenity by a U.S. citizen on one of our public broadcasting stations, and the letters came in mostly negative. A lot of people wanted to know why it was that such a mean-spirited man with such a hostile hand was allowed to remain at large. Wasn't there a law for locking up such monsters and freaks? Other viewers thought that this Bill guy, while maybe he talked dirty, was still, when properly equipped, probably the most efficient cleaning human ever known. And so while the public debated the advisability of letting people with enormous hands wander the streets swearing into microphones and shaking their gigantic fists at an otherwise peaceable and inoffensive citizenry, a few calls came to Bill's private telephone from people wondering just what could possibly be Bill's fee to clean and deodorize their homes, and Bill, angered and hurt by hints that he was a dirty guy, came to terms with these queries and pledged his cleaning services. Now called to public commercial duty, he resigned his post as Chief Checkout Operator and Bagger of the Schnuck's supermarket chain, leaving various world records for checking out and bagging prowess safely inaccessible to other mortals. He added a vacuuming unit to his backpack and ran a hose down his arm and under one big finger, so he was ready to handle almost any kind of mess humans could make.

Thus began a relatively happy period in Bill's life. He cleaned and deodorized many filthy homes. Nevertheless, he was still getting a bum rap in the press as investigative reporters uncovered a past filled with obscenities, injured playmates, and the occasional crushed food item at Schnuck's. Meanwhile, some of his more well meaning/meddlesome cleaning customers suggested he might apologize to the people for broadcasting dirty words and so earn their good opinion, but Bill resented such advice. Was he supposed to let that reporter make fun of him? His customers then warned him to "watch your back" and "look out," for anti-Bill forces were taking *their* resentment to the streets.

And in fact, citizen patrols were performing sweeps in the city streets around Bill's house and in the nearby wealthy gated neighborhood where many of Bill's cleaning customers resided. The patrols were loosely organized by an employee of the private security company that prowled in tiny ACME Security Services pickup trucks, keeping all brands of riffraff at a distance, such employee claiming to represent the large balance of gated residents who didn't think such a dangerous cleaner should have an unregulated right of way on their private streets.

One such sweep caught Bill walking home after an especially furious day of cleaning. He heard someone tapping on his backpack, turned around, and found several red-faced people who wanted to know why he was wearing that backpack and did he have a permit to dispense liquified cleaning agents, and did he know that utilizing a cleaning agent in a manner inconsistent with its labeling was legally actionable, potentially tortious, and why was his one hand so big, and didn't he know that a single swear word heard at the wrong time in a child's development could throw a monkey wrench into the slick gears of that child's moral reasoning and drive a wedge between that child and his or her parents and produce excessive anxiety in the Home, and didn't he have any values of common decency or fellow feeling for his fellow people?

All this rhetorical criticism compelled Bill to raise his hands as if to call a time out. But the act of raising his enormous hand with all its tubes and attachments gleaming and glinting in the streetlight like the sights and barrels of a really advanced gun, this hand at the end of a long and muscular arm grown thick from putting scouring force at the hand's disposal, such act of hand-raising frightened those amateur vigilantes into a defensive and somewhat frenzied state, which in certain cases involved screaming, such screaming seeming to summon an ACME Security Services pickup truck, its logo and distinguishing marks cunningly concealed, out of which sprang the loose organizer, two off-duty cops, and a lanky kid brother out for a firsthand taste of public discipline to help him in his career decision. This gang of four rushed defensively yet aggressively to the scene, and it was these newcomers who fell upon Bill first, and then there was a fracas and a general piling on.

In the crush and panic, one man brandished a knife. This man had no particular grudge against Bill, yet he carried, like a mole on his forehead, a tendency to harm in search of a motive, such motive amply supplied by the mini-mob, which, for its part, lacked a strong offensive impulse, such complementary mingling of motives and propensities making a recipe for violence, i.e., this man tried to stab Bill's hand. At first Bill felt Dawn dishwashing liquid running down his wrist and liquid Comet cleanser puddling in his palm. Then he smelled Pine Sol eating a wound in his hand, filling the air with a fresh lemony scent. All the while, he whipped his assailant around on the palm of his hand, working that attacker back and forth and revolving in the air like a car on the Scrambler, until that addled slasher made a clean stab directly into Bill's hand.

As Bill wailed in pain, the mini-mob came to its senses. They paused and collectively thought that maybe they had gone too far and should certainly turn back right now, but then it appeared that the roller coaster of violence was only just slowing at the top of its first great hill, so their potential energy for malicious action was maximized, and then did it roll: Bill's large arm was held against the sidewalk by several citizens, and the enormous hand was cut off and taken away by the people. Bill was left, bruised and bloodied and with but one hand, lying on his backpack, his various tubes leaking blood and cleaning agents of all kinds, including pure water. As his blood ran out of him, so did his consciousness. Luckily, a nice person soon arrived on the scene and cleverly tied his belt around Bill's forearm and called an ambulance, which came, and they took Bill to the hospital and revived him and saved him from death.

Meanwhile, in a nearby alley, the amateur vigilantes got appalled at each other and leveled many intramural accusations regarding activities such as assault, mayhem, amputation, and chance-medley. The ACME Security Services pickup truck quietly returned to its gated jurisdiction, its occupants shedding false mustaches, sideburns, beards, wigs, glasses, platform boots, and brightly colored sweaters, all such disguises disposed of discreetly. The severed hand passed among the remaining citizens like a medicine ball until the cagey and cop-fearing couple of Ken and Peggy Bergstrom decided that the sooner they removed the hand from the alley and disbanded the better. They climbed into their Nissan Sentra, put the bloody hand in the child seat, and raced home, trying to guess the plot of *Cut It Out, Rob!* for alibi purposes. When they arrived home, the show turned out to be a rerun, and they were so relieved that they gave the babysitter a huge tip.

After the show ended, they went to the garage to examine the enormous hand. It seemed that the thing to do would be to get rid of it, but they resisted this decision for the longest time, staring at the hand, which was becoming stiff and sticky with congealed blood and viscous cleaning agents. Without a word between them, Peggy covered it in plastic wrap and placed it in the freezer in the garage, pending a final disposal strategy.

With the hand safely stowed, Peggy finally burst into tears. Her husband blinked in sympathetic and tremulous emotion, but found assuagement for his queasy feelings in certain memories of public swearing and heavy-handed menacing. He declared, "It serves that bastard right. Swearing in front of our child."

"He was a monster," she sobbed.

They filed into the house and washed their hands.

* * *

A lot of public remorse and hand-wringing took place over the prairie justice that had been wreaked on Bill. A TV station that had been scooped the first time around tried for an interview with Bill, but would he please not swear because if he kept it clean he could tell his case to the entire world. Bill did not promise anything, and at that moment broke into the sort of mean-spirited swearing that nobody likes to hear. Bill's customers sent him bouquets of flowers and descriptions of how their homes were going to hell in a hand-basket without his enormous hand to take care of things, but Bill didn't feel up to feeling many feelings of thankfulness, much less dictating a nice reply or two even to these well-meaning people for their valuable support.

Right about this time, Bill was visited in the hospital by an old flame of his by the name of Linda Talck. Linda Talck's guiding characteristic was an inordinate interest in other people's private business, and she had been attracted to Bill because she suspected he might have a lot of psychological problems she could service. Bill and Linda dated a single time. Things did not go well at the drive-in. For starters, there was Talck's confession that she'd been in some pretty bad relationships where she lost respect for herself and her partner, and she hoped that she and Bill would communicate a lot and never lie to each other and be really open with each other, like when she was little and her parents were still together and it was OK to walk around naked all the time and only close doors for silence and never privacy. "Including the bathroom!" Talck exclaimed with an excited, self-congratulating laugh. Bill imagined Talck standing in front of him, yammering while he tried to take a shit, and right there, at the drive-in, he began to perspire through all of his skin.

Then, as Talck segued from her happy nudist childhood to the dark days of The Pre-Divorce, The Divorce, and The Post-Divorce, while the ignored movie played, surreal and distant, occasionally filling the car with bursts of kaleidoscopic subconscious dialogue, Bill had a flashback: his tall and strong mother picked up his midget father and hurled him onto a cot blanketed with an orange and white parachute silk that his father was strangely fond of and liked to have near him and to take naps within. And under this combined onslaught of communication and memory, Bill's breathing became shallow and rapid, and he felt a desperate defensive urge to bite Talck's tongue. Such urge was not sexual per se, yet as he moved his teeth into biting range and Talck reflexively offered him her tongue, motives got tangled and passionate lip-biting and French-kissing and full-scale petting ensued. But Bill soon horrified himself when his efforts to slip his right hand under Talck's bra succeeded in bursting the cups right off her breasts, so that his caress suddenly resembled Godzilla barging through Tokyo. To Bill, that is. Because Linda, though she was alarmed by Bill's destruction of her bra, nevertheless found his touch surprisingly deft, and she put both of her hands on his hand as if to give encouragement and guidance to his explorations. Bill misinterpreted her clutching of his hand (and her passionate groans) as a terrified attempt to remove or control the hand, and, self-repulsed, he bolted from the car, jumped the fence of the drive-in, and ran home.

Yet Talck did not hold this against him. She expressed her eagerness to work through Bill's issues, sending him notes on the theme "We have to talk." But Bill was scared, unsettled by Talck's fascination with his problems, as if she were turned on by his grotesque hand and unstable behavior, so he ended their romantic relationship.

Years had passed since then, punctuated with sporadic Talck encounters. Sometimes she would be very cheerful and positive about her life, hoping to draw Bill into her happy world; sometimes she would be depressed and tearful, trying to get Bill to pity her; sometimes she chided Bill about his lack of emotional development. "You've got to love your hand, Bill," she said, but Bill only wondered if this meant she had heard those old schoolyard taunts about the likely connection between the size of his hand and an especially demanding masturbation regimen.

So now here was Talck, braless in a blue turtleneck and bell-bottom jeans, walking right into his hospital room to be with him in his time of need and weakness. She took a seat and said to him, "Are you OK?"

Bill wanted to say "Fuck you," but he also didn't want to say it.

Linda said, "I know you're in a difficult place right now. That's OK. Sometimes it's OK to be in a difficult place."

Bill remembered why he used to like her, which was also why she tended to enrage him: she was ready to talk about emotional problems, about personal and intimate issues, and Bill had a huge need to talk about such things. But when she talked, his bullshit detector flashed and beeped. Plus he considered her concern for him the tip of an iceberg, the immense submerged base of which was her desire that he be concerned about her, a desire that Bill was emotionally unequipped to gratify and one that he resented since it was not straightforward. Even now, as he was tempted to accept her sympathy at face value, his old judgment kept asserting itself. This tension made Bill extremely irritable and mean, far beyond what the current situation seemed to warrant, and because he felt that the greater danger lay in yielding to the quick emotional hand job she seemed willing to administer, he growled, "Get the hell out."

Linda said, "I know you're angry. That's OK."

"Get the fuck out!"

Linda let this hang in the air, unanswered, as absolute proof that he was being mean to her when all she was trying to do was show that she cared, but this wasn't surprising, as she had always been treated this way by everyone she had ever loved. She cried quietly by his bedside for ten minutes, while Bill pretended to sleep, while in fact his head almost exploded from bottled rage and guilt and a nagging sense that Talck had the right idea on some level. Finally, Linda rested a hand on his shoulder, then left his room.

Now Bill really began to wonder about himself and his inability to return affection and his bitterness, and there, in his hospital bed, he performed many devastating acts of self-analysis whereby he decided that he really knew who he was, and who he was was a guy who either had nothing emotionally to do with people or wanted to crush them and break their bones, such coldness or hostility precluding the good relations people sometimes had with each other. Thus did Bill create for himself sensations of deep funk and self-pity, in such bathtub of feeling did he try to drown—until at night came vivid dreams in which he scoured the countryside with an even larger and more ferocious hand, which would lay all of his enemies low, but when Bill woke up it was he who had been laid low, and he didn't feel very good about it.

About this time, a plastic surgeon came by with some sketches for Bill to peruse, for this surgeon would like to build Bill a brand new prosthetic hand that would be even bigger and better than the big flesh hand he used to have. Instead of awkward tubes strapped on with duct tape, this new hand would have tubes built right in, with push-button cleaning agent selection and microchip-regulated Flow Control, and at the fingertips there would be assorted brushes and sponges and other cleaning tools. Bill's heart and self-perception rebounded, until he found out the procedure would cost more than $300,000—a significant percentage of which would not be covered by his Personal Insurance Plan because of the allegedly "elective" nature of the hand's design.

But Bill's hope-fueled fires still burned, so at last he made courtesy calls to those rich flower-senders, speaking openly of his prosthetic dream. Lo and behold, some of those loyal customers were of the philanthropic persuasion and threw together fund-raising dinners and charity balls and celebrity golf tournaments the way other people get up teams for playground basketball, and they duly proclaimed a benefit dance to benefit Bill's hand so he could resume his rightful place as a very clean and cleansing member of the community.

However, the anti-Bill lobby, scattered and somewhat shamed in the aftermath of the Bill attack, cautiously regrouped and reminded everyone of the swearing that had brought this monster to the public's attention in the first place—and how the real truth of everything was that Bill had attacked those people and the hand was severed self-defensively. They also lobbied the city council that this violated a certain provision of the Public Cleaners Code, and that Bill had never had a properly stamped Public Cleaners License. A few people even researched the Sherman Antitrust Act and found that the merger of Bill's five market-leading fingers in one hand constituted a "massive combination" and an "unfair restraint of trade" destined to drive all other cleaners out of business and threaten consumers with the specter of monopolistic pricing. And letters to the media asked whether we were ready for a bionic man, whether Frankenstein was a good role model for our kids, and what was wrong with a normal-sized hand, or even the time-honored hook? This anxiety-driven sentiment tended to wash hard against those who simply felt that it would be neat to have a guy with a real powerful hand for cleaning, and the great tilt of the public mood began to weigh against Bill.

Meanwhile, the skittish and threatened plastic surgeon raised Bill's fee fifty grand, demanded round-the-clock police protection, got fitted for a bulletproof vest, and sewed lead into his pants. Then, on a crisp evening, it just so happened that all the rolls of crepe paper that were to be strung from the ceiling of the charity ball were stolen and ignited in a hilltop conflagration. And spray-painted on overpasses were messages such as "Beware MacHand," and one day a nimble airplane drew a smoky hand against the sky, sparking hope in the watching Bill until this airplane circumscribed the area at great speed and then soared slantwise across the dissolving hand.

Thus could Bill see which way the wind was blowing, and daily he discussed the matter with his stump, though he imagined he spoke with the hand, his painful funk having metamorphosed via ebbing hopes into looniness and delusional states. Even his rich benefit-throwing friends wondered if the massive anti-Bill tide could be successfully breasted, and some went ahead on the sly to hire other cleaners at reduced rates, and the person who was supposed to replace the crepe paper never got around to it. So by the time Bill was released from the hospital, having rejected a common

wood and latex prosthesis in his general wackiness and residual de-
nial, he lacked support.

When he returned to his small home, he found a giant hand
burned in the tiny lawn and effigies of hands in his bushes and his
mailbox, along with a pile of mannequin hands by his front door.
Squirrels had invaded Bill's house through a broken window. He
faced a big mess, and he was hung briefly between an impulse to
laugh and an impulse to cry. He decided to laugh extremely hard
right away and thus triumph over the situation with his great and
superior humor, but the laugh he embarked upon was of a fine, low
intensity, as if his impulse to laugh were a garden hose with a tight
nozzle. So he laughed a fine mist for several days, such misty laugh
nurturing the green grimness of the situation rather than drown-
ing such grimness as a larger, more fluent laugh might have done.
While the laugh malfunctioned, Bill could do nothing but start
cleaning and ordering his house and yard, such work as might suck
out of him any hope of ever doing anything else, for never could
this all be done with a mere one regular-sized hand.

But then who should pass by one day in her Nissan Sentra but
Peggy Bergstrom. After the detaching, transporting in the child seat,
and freezing of the hand, she had become progressively remorseful,
even as her husband's anger simmered and spattered. A few days
before, he had claimed that three-year-old Benjamin had become
a holy terror since hearing a certain swear word on TV and, sure,
what they'd done was drastic but so was Hiroshima, and so were
the Rosenberg executions, and so was—but he apparently ran out
of such examples and turned to the *Cut It Out, Rob!* alibi, to which
Peggy responded that strictly because the program was a rerun it
was of no use to them, and at this he declared that now he'd heard

everything. Peggy then described how much she would appreciate it if he didn't shout at her, but Ken claimed that he wasn't shouting, and so did their discussion bog down on the exact definition of shouting.

Later that night, Peggy had gone out to the freezer to look at the hand. It scared her, for it seemed the hand of a mighty giant who might come and slay her, but she put this thought out of her head, but her sleeping dreams were filled with threatening digits that closed python-like around her throat and clasped elephant-like around her waist and insinuated man-like between her thighs and poked her Stooge-like in the eyes: this was the five-fingered grip of fear and memory and longing and guilt and pain in which the severed hand held her consciousness.

Trying to escape such thoughts, she would hit the road in her Sentra, yet she was predictably drawn back to Bill's neighborhood and the scene of the crime. Thus on this day she saw Bill in his yard trying to pull toilet paper from the tree with a rake, the rake just then toppling to earth in the lame grip of Bill's left hand. It occurred to her that she might perform a drive-by confession right at that moment, from the safety of her car, and she powered down the passenger side window and leaned over to do so, but what she actually said was: "Excuse me, I'm lost, can you tell me how to get to the zoo?"

Frustrated with his rake, Bill answered, "Fuck you!"

Instead of being mortified by his swear word, Peggy was puzzled by the odd grin breaking Bill's face while he made his lips say "Suck my stump"—still she thought she saw the soul of forgiveness behind his eyes. But when he approached the car and stuffed his stump through the passenger window and lunged a good deal of himself after it and said, "I remember you," she screamed and hit the gas and dragged Bill down the street until she realized what she was doing and stopped the car. She darted over to him and said, yes, it was her and she was sorry.

Peggy then lugged Bill's body by the armpits out of the street and onto his gasoline-scarred lawn. She was going to call an ambulance, but Bill cursed the hospital and all its minions and instead asked for a simple bandage to stanch the seeping wound on his right leg.

And just like in a movie, the repentant Peggy cleaned the wound on Bill's knee and thigh. This wound was not as bad as first expected since the dragging was brief and Bill's Levi's blue jeans offered protection, yet nevertheless did Peggy spend some time sponging the wounds and tweezing bits of gravel and road grit from them. During this painstaking operation, Bill resisted the urge to administer a retaliatory gripping with his left hand or a vengeful blow with his stump, and, as he resisted, Peggy's care and apologies blew away the smoke of his rage and the preexisting fog of his aggressive looniness, leaving behind a sudden stark intimacy, which embarrassed both of them. After the bandaging, Bill asked to be excused and sat alone in his bedroom for five minutes, recovering from the shock to his leg and to his privacy, this personal center inadvertently abraded by the caring contact of the apologizing hand-severer-and-freezer named Peggy.

As Bill repaired his personal boundaries, Peggy tried to calm herself by viewing the everyday objects in his living room. On closer inspection, Bill's coffee table appeared covered with dirty, squirrel-sized footprints, an observation that made Peggy wonder if Bill was a weirdo who harbored strange pets. Before her anxiety could crest into panic, Bill emerged from his bedroom and said he was all right and was thankful to her for tweezing and dressing his wound. He regretted the appearance of his living room and described how vandalism had led to an invasion of squirrels, the signs of which he was still working to efface. Such apologies and explanations elicited from Peggy further professions of remorse for everything she had ever done or thought against him, but Bill waved his stump dismissively and turned the conversation to the incremental improvements his left hand was achieving as a cleaning tool. At this moment Peggy was moved to say, "But I still have your big hand! It's frozen! It may still work!"

Bill had no time for skepticism. He instantly posited his next goal in life: the reattachment and return to functioning of his original hand. He said it was immediately necessary to see his frozen hand, and Peggy said this was sort of a problem, since it was in the freezer in her garage and her husband was unfortunately not as pro-Bill as she was, and so they arranged to meet in her garage in the wee hours.

And this was done. Bill arrived early in the middle of a night that would leave thick dew on the lawns of the region. He huddled on the cement walk that ran behind the garage. Finally he received the signal, stepped through the back door, and found Peggy bent over the large white Deepfreeze, removing with two hands a heavy object that if Bill hadn't known it for his own mitt, he might have mistaken it for a tom turkey, of such a hue and mass did it seem. Bill cradled his detached hand with his left hand, his stomach performing acts of main support, while his stump caressed through the plastic the strands of cleaning tubes and felt the frozen puddles of leaked cleaning agents. Pieces of sponge and brush stuck out here and there, and it was his hand, and his own blood was upon it. The

stump throbbed with recognition, trembling like the tail-wagging
of a dog upon seeing its delinquent master after a stretch. Peggy
shed a few tears, finding her trough of remorseful feelings to be an
undrainable swamp, while Bill, wrestling with his own composure,
asked her to keep the hand safe for him. He wasn't sure that his own
frost-choked refrigerator's freezing compartment could accommodate the hand—would she keep it pending arrangements for reattachment?

And this time Bill was a bit more shrewd about publicity. He held
a press conference in which he announced that one of his assailants had confessed, and he, a clean and upstanding young man, was
not the sort to hold a grudge. He said he understood momentary
bursts of rage, even tightly nozzled rage with a fine, misty intensity.
Thus he granted good feelings of forgiveness to all his assailants,
including and especially the one who might still have his intact
hand, which he naturally hoped that person would offer to his doctors by calling the confidential hotline number on the bottom of
the screen. And, by the way, would everyone from now on please
think of him as a basically clean and good person who never meant
to use his big hand to any unfair advantage, except maybe to gain
the loyal patronage of his cleaning customers, but this was after all
pursuant to his god-given American right to perform his role in the
efficient division of the world's labor, such division being an engine
of wealth and prosperity, globally—in other words, could everyone
remember that the hand was just good for cleaning?

Bill's statement went on for some time, some several centuries
of local TV time, and though only an elliptic and mangled version
of his statement was shown to the viewers, Bill preferred to think
he had made a perfectly clean public breast of it, and so he began

creatively visualizing the successful reattachment and return to functioning of his beloved hand.

Now the doctors determined that of the eight carpal bones that constitute the wrist, the three-cornered triquetrum was crushed, the navicular was cracked, the lunate was gouged, and the pisiform was shivered; of the other four carpal bones, the capitate and the trapezoid and the hamate were unscathed, and the trapezium was nicked yet serviceable. The challenge for the doctors was to manufacture high-density plastic replacement bones (made with 10 percent real bone particles), of precise dimension and everlasting lubricity, to assure successful articulation with Bill's intact radius and ulna. And as for the muscles, the cordy ends of the abductor pollicis longus and the extensor pollicis brevis and the extensor digitorum and the extensor digiti minimi and other such muscles would have to be sewn with lasers to their attaching nodes in the severed hand and likewise with the threading of certain crucial nerves, which, being rather touchy, shall remain nameless. Similarly would the doctors reconnect the ulnar artery and the radial artery and the digital arteries and the palmar arch, along with their veinal counterparts.

Thus under bright lamps and a blanket of insurance coverage did Bill lie down to be operated on. The operation was conducted over a thirty-six-hour period and required two teams of twelve specialists, the entire medical unit working very hard to turn Latin names into functioning parts of the human body. It was said that more than four gallons of sweat were perspired by the attending doctors and three and three-quarters gallons of sweat were lost by the attending nurses; inversely, Bill's body drank seven and one-half pints of type O blood. The final and most significant thing said about the operation was that, yes, it seemed to work, and if Physical Therapy

could pick up the ball very gingerly and run with it very lightly, Bill
might regain the functioning of his enormous hand as if it were as
good as new.

* * *

Meanwhile, full-scale hostilities broke out at the Bergstrom resi-
dence as young Benjamin ate too much chalk and had to be rushed
to the emergency room. Ken accused Peggy of motherly delinquency
and also of being a bad example, such accusations sparking a three-
and-a-half-hour shouting match in which—via freewheeling his-
torical allusions, direct quotations, and pungent paraphrases—they
created an oral anthology of every argument they had ever had.

Yet this argument was almost a relief in the context of Ken's recent conversational habits, which consisted of repeated and strenu-
ous references to the hand-severing incident as "drastic but necessary," though these references brought Ken no peace, since rather
than mixing and canceling each other out, necessity floated like
an oil slick on a great ocean of drasticness, such insolubility pro-
moting Ken's tendency to bitch and recriminate, such insolubility
persisting in the face of Bill's stirring offer of amnesty as well as
news of his operation and his jones for physical therapy. Peggy suggested that Ken was simply suffering from post-traumatic stress
disorder—amputation was a stressful act, not to mention the guilt.
But Ken fired back that they were *both* guilty, notwithstanding her
traitorous return of the amputated hand, which silenced Peggy,
who was afraid to reveal her secret contacts with Bill and claimed
to have returned the hand solely because she had been moved by
Bill's dramatic televised plea.

Their bickerings only exacerbated the derangement of Benjamin, who as soon as his stomach had been pumped chalk-free was always climbing on top of things and threatening to throw himself down, and breaking the breakable, and gnashing his teeth, and who, in one great gesture of almost unbelievable dirtiness, dropped trou and defecated in the sandbox at the day-care center. Faced with such actions, even mild-mannered parents might be moved to drastic but necessary acts of discipline, whereas the Bergstroms saw in their own hands the potential for a brutal and thorough and possibly unstoppable beating of Benjamin. Peggy reasoned to herself that violence was a habit that broke and could not be broken, unless entire personalities were revamped. In the meantime, the Bergstroms stopped recycling, let their shrubs grow wild, bid recklessly at bridge, and kept each other freshly lacerated with sharp words and salty oaths, such that Peggy wondered if she could endure her household any longer.

This domestic chaos led her to make another trip to Bill's house, which she found sparkling clean and utterly restored. When she rang the bell, she was greeted by a Bill who seemed glad and surprised to see her, but in the instant before he recognized her, she detected a green gloom hanging like a tarp over his face. Feeling an intimacy that could only have come from assaulting him and cutting off his hand and dragging him by her car and tweezing bits of gravel and road grit from his thigh and plotting reattachment with him, she asked what was wrong. Bill was reluctant to say and instead offered to get lemonade while she might take a seat in the living room. As he scooped dry lemonade granules from a huge cylindrical container, Peggy happened to see the Cleaning Agent

Dispenser Backpack in a corner. When Bill returned, bearing lemonade, she offhandedly asked him when he was going to resume
his position as a clean and cleansing member of the community. He
said it was funny she should mention this, because before she had
arrived he had been considering that very question.

Peggy sensibly observed that reattachment afforded him a choice
of careers: he could take up his backpack and clean, or return to
Schnuck's, or blaze an entirely new trail. Bill said she was theoreti-
cally right, but then he mumbled that somehow reattachment had
not blossomed into the total happiness he had anticipated. When
gently pressed, he elaborated on his funk in the hospital, during
which he had acknowledged his inability to have normal and productive relations with his fellow humans and saw how various fears,
resentments, suspicions, and rages were blocking love and clogging
his affection ports and channels. He had expected this mood to dissipate upon reattachment, and sometimes he did feel better, yet still
now did he realize that he was himself after all, and this was not
necessarily to be borne on account of certain feelings having to do
with the monstrosity of his hand, however cleansing or profitable,
having to do with his lingering fears and resentments, having to do
with the general mystery of his self, a mystery made all too apparent during his days of handlessness and delusion and yet probably
brought home most forcefully by reattachment, for when he held
up his hand to look at it and become reacquainted with its profile,
this enormous hand curved into a question mark, such suggestive
shape graphically positing the riddle of *Just what was a human hand
for?* Now that he could use it to clean and deodorize again, providing
such services appeared to him trivial and even degrading, reducing
him to a mere hired hand in the conspiracy of cleanliness, by which

proxies for real human dirtiness were swept up and scrubbed down and flushed away, while real human dirtiness flourished. And yet to forsake cleaning and return to Schnuck's, or to undertake some new direction, meant turning his back on the one substantial gift he possessed.

Despite his acquaintance with Linda Talck, Bill had never felt so free to reveal his concerns, and thus they spilled from him quickly and prodigiously. Yet he worried that the unbelievable quantity of emotional dirt he had thrown at Peggy would certainly repulse her right into the next century.

In fact Peggy had to take a moment to absorb the speech of this enormously handed man, but what seeped through the wall of his self-analysis, thrown up like a row of sandbags against a rising river, was the sense that he had become warped and anxious from the sort of loneliness that deformity and bitterness too often produce. The state of loneliness struck an especially responsive chord in Peggy, because she also suffered from a version of this feeling, even in the midst of marriage and family. And thus by some trick, or miracle, of empathetic imagination, Peggy's problems seemed to overlap perfectly with those of Bill, a coincidence that moved her. Then there was Bill himself, sitting in a stuffed chair, his body sunken and diminished by emotional emission, his big hand free of gadgetry and resting palm up on the arm of the chair like an obedient dog. And there she was, on the sofa, leaning toward the man she had formerly seen as a monster. She took his enormous hand in hers.

At this time Bill's hand began to heat like batter pressed between the flanks of a waffle iron. He watched her touching of him with a great big face on his head, probably the biggest face he had ever had, and he felt as though his eyes would liquefy and run down his face.

Then Peggy's waffling touch turned into a tentative two-handed ex-
ploratory massage of the massive base of his thumb, during which
she recalled how she had wrapped and entombed this very hand in
her freezer. Yet rather than ride the uncanny notion of resurrected
flesh over metaphysical mountains and theological deserts and
symbolical valleys, she strove to stay in touch with the driver of
such ramblings: the hand itself, the driving physicality of the hand
itself.

And so she worked outward from the great trough of palm along
untraveled roads—his life line, his head line, his heart line, his
health line. Bill's breathing suggested these creases had a sensitiv-
ity reserved for erogenous zones and the better nerves of the body,
and so Peggy ran her thumbnail down these creases, cleaning the
hand the way certain nerves need to be cleaned so that they may
hum like strung and plucked copper wires and the finer gut wires
of the inner human network of feeling. Such crease and nerve cleaning complete, she moved on to his tremendous fingers and their
phalanges of bone and muscle. She playfully cracked his knuckles,
the tender burstings of fluid nodes within the knuckles somehow
producing a bursting of fluid nodes within Bill's eyes, for her caress
had brought him to a great plain of emotion. His liquefying eyes
began to weep openly. The sheer delight in witnessing human emotion made Peggy laugh, and Bill followed her into laughter, erupt-
ing in great spastic coughing laughs like a spigot whose supplying
pipes have hung unused for a long time. His hiccupy laughs, which
seemed both to delight him and to cause him pain, in turn brought
tears to Peggy's eyes. Thus together they trekked through deep
valleys of crying and high peaks of laughing, oscillating so that
their waves canceled into a straight line of humming feeling that

yet gathered intensity like a rolling snowball gathers mass until it seemed to both of them that the hand was swollen with an unbelievable concentration of energy unheard of in the history of hands or in the history of all human body parts.

Now let it be accepted that the mechanics of human copulation and reproduction are well known. Even mildly perspicacious preteens have been seen casually sketching a uterus and its rack of fallopian tubes, or lecturing one another on the functioning of the vas deferens or the seminal vesicles. Peggy, being a wife and mother, certainly knew these matters inside and out, while Bill had done the deed in the employees' bathroom at Schnuck's with the wise-cracking, chunky checker from neighboring aisle seven, who merely asked was it true what they said about the size of a man's hand. But despite their all-too-detailed knowledge of how they might mate, sexual frankness developed between Bill and Peggy without proceeding down those well-worn paths. Instead, Peggy's tremendous hand job now included an increasingly insistent use of Bill's hand as a rubbing site to be visited by the erogenous zones of her own body, zones like pilgrims in progression—a cheek, her neck, a breast. Though he felt an impulse to respond to this sexual shift, Bill did not move his hand. He simply kept it there and was with her with it in the same way as before.

Let it also be known quite directly that such ham-handed contact evolved, through ardent rubbing and strategic disrobing, into a bout of digital intercourse between Bill and Peggy, with Peggy on top and the hand on the bottom on the arm of the chair. And without getting unnecessarily explicit, let it also be known that the finger chosen by Bill and Peggy for this passionate act was Bill's right ring finger, probably the most sacred and important finger on his

entire hand; and let it also be known (without going into the sort
of detail that might violate community standards or otherwise run
afoul of Chief Justice Warren Burger's opinion in *Miller v. California*)
that during such digital union Peggy made gutteral moaning noises
that humans cannot actually make, that through skillful and delicate maneuvering and Bill's passive holding steady she achieved
orgasm, a tremendous shuddering from deep within her that was
answered by an involuntary shudder from the enormous hand, that
her shuddering from deep within was, for Bill, preceded by the sensation of a ring of flesh tightening on his ring finger.

Let us also tiptoe over to the fact that after all this shuddering,
Bill had the sense of coming back to himself after having been miss-
ing, and found her still there, still tremulous and moving upon
him, and still reaching for something, though something going or
coming he couldn't tell. Once again he thought of moving, though
his stillness had allowed him to hold incredible amounts of energy
in his palm, enough energy to commit fission, a concentration that
even a tremendous shuddering could not dissipate or keep from
growing.

Finally, an intense longing plus a fear of implosion plus a brute
need to be there more added up to a circuit-busting conviction in
the pit of his brain: he must move within her or he would die. Now,
too, this narration must venture into a new degree of explicitness
or risk its own death, and thus will clearly state that there within
her his finger was at the center of the drop of velvety liquid feeling that was the whole room and probably the entire englobed
world, so he had to be careful here for one false move could strike
her into something different and separate and dead and looking at
him for his motives and assumptions. Yet there was certain death in

not moving, at this point, and to be always at this point was some kind of painful ideal. Then he moved by crooking slightly the top two joints of his thick ring finger, hooking her to him as she almost rose up and left him. Peggy seemed to think his gesture was OK, yet still, with his finger slightly hooking, he felt like a golfer who has launched a towering nine-iron shot straight at the flag yet doesn't know where it will land, exactly.

But it was Peggy who landed, and soon. Her slowed rhythm stopped. Bill wondered whether his finger movement was unwanted or belated or beside the point, but he told himself he did actually move and hook her to himself in an active gesture of love, if only she knew such was its meaning. Still sitting on his palm, she threw her feet behind her and collapsed onto his chest, her hair falling forward with all of her falling forward onto him. Her breath was like a rancid paste and his breath was similar. She breathed against him and their fiery-hot cheeks breathed against each other. Finally, she kissed him on the cheek and renewed her fall against him. Deep within herself she felt him wiggle the tip of his thick finger. In her ear he whispered, "Hello."

There was a new and strange tone in this word, which moved her to lift herself from his chest and look closely into his face and eyes. Whether he meant to say anything else or not, he seemed just then unable to speak and to be uncomfortable with not being able to speak. His breathing picked up, such that its rancid spiciness swept into her nose like wind, and while she tried to compose a countergreeting, she made a mental note to tell him gently at the right moment something to the effect of, if they ever did this again, maybe he—no, "they," say "they"—they might think about using some clean and deodorizing mouthwash so that when they ever shared this beautiful act again, it would smell even better.

As the storm of their feelings moved on and the urgency went out of their silent look at each other, he decided that his hooking and subsequent wiggle, considered as one gesture, was probably the best thing he had ever done. It occurred to him that he might never clean with his hand again (for suddenly the hand itself seemed so clean, so appropriate), that a hand was mainly for touching, that a hand worked best when its touch took you inside another person. He fought with his need to tell her this, lugging this observation and its accompanying profession of love from his mind to his lips.

But in the lugging of "I love you" there was a terrible attrition of subject and object and verb, due to guerrilla attacks by a residual sense of self-monstrosity and boy/girl diffidence, egged on by the slightly receding stiffening of her neck and the almost impercep- tible look of distaste on her face when she pulled away after their faces had been so close, such stiffening rearming the ragtag rem- nants of resentment and bitterness, such that when "I love you" ar- rived at its destination, it had been raided and reduced to a residue of mere address, just the word "Hello," again.

The oddity of his strained double-greeting intensified Peggy's fight with familiar and new feelings from a world ungoverned by the driving physicality of the hand, feelings that rushed in as the hand's physicality receded. Could she tell him that to ride with her in the hot-air balloon of love he might just clean up his act, mean- ing more than his breath, meaning maybe also the whitewashing of what she feared was a constitutional green gloom, were it possible? For the sense that he might be psychologically unwell was growing on her—even as she was aware how his adulterous digit pricked her own tender and unstable and violent psyche. His personal growth she might watch or even aid, rather at a distance, from the precarious hiding place of her marriage, until she was more sure of him, or at least of her strength to share her acts with his, for with the returning memory of her marriage came an enormous sense of the stakes of her behavior and of the need for certainty in her loving relationships. But could she maybe love him in between? But couldn't she maybe accept him for what he was? It was hard to know, yet she knew she wanted to feel more right and absolutely touched in her love. She could imagine that now.

Instead of saying any of this, she said, "That was wonderful."

"That was wonderful," he repeated, as if learning how to speak.

"It was," she affirmed, and knew she wasn't lying.

She gingerly slipped off the hand and stood there, and they exchanged sheepish smiles. Bill's head roared with the word "wonderful" and the words "it was" and again "wonderful." He took a deep and proud breath. "I'm sweaty," he said, and laughed nervously.

"Let's get you in the shower, then," she said. She blushed because she thought her distaste for his smell was showing.

"You'll come in with me?" he asked, and he marveled at how intimate this would be. If she had been impressed with his enormous hand as a sexual tool, what would she think when it was cleaning her? This was the only type of cleaning Bill wanted to do for the rest of his life.

Now Peggy was blushing even more, because would climbing into the shower with him involve real sex? Or had they already had real sex?

"Do you think we know each other well enough to shower together?" she joked.

"You're right," he said, seriously. "Maybe when we clean each other—we should, really—it should be a commitment, don't you think?" Already he was speaking the language of intimacy, and he congratulated himself. He had never been so serious.

She would have laughed, but he was so painfully intent on loving her, on wanting to love her exactly right. It was almost too much—his hand, his smell, his overwhelming loving intent. She had to know that he wouldn't destroy her somehow, that inside, beyond his smell and his huge obscene soiled hand, he was of her kind; she had to be sure, above all, that he was *nice*. She would consider accepting him, she proposed to herself, as soon as he was clean. She took his enormous hand and led him to the shower.

O n Tuesday we got an overwhelming urge to see California. We had a red Honda Civic hatchback. We filled it with gas and got on I-70. Westbound. 10:51 AM.

The road went on for miles. And it was not the most distinctive road. But by paying careful attention, we saw the country change its face. Oh, the dips and hillocks of Kansas. Can a land have a haunch? Can you swing a cat in rural Missouri without hitting another person swinging a cat in rural Missouri? But what did we know about America? Even less than we knew about ourselves, I'm sure. We weren't taking a road trip—we were *fleeing.*

Julie had quit her systems job at the local phone monopoly after a cataclysmic project management debacle, and I was one of those eighth-year history grad students on the borderline between plausible and department joke. Summer had hit and St. Louis felt soaked in lighter fluid. A couple of a different kidney might have headed north into, say, darkest Minnesota, with a tent, a bag of marshmallows, and a few tubes of edible lubricant, but the California clichés had overrun our flabby imaginations and directed our balding tires westward.

It was sunny. Our road attitude was pure: Julie with bare feet out the window, reading Deepak Chopra's *Return of the Rishi;* me with one hand on the wheel, the other fingering the freeway breeze, slaloming around trucks and families in minivans watching TV, old couples in Cadillacs clogging the left lane out of a lifelong sense of achievement and privilege, young solo females in Neons and Aleros who we decided had majored in marketing and/or communications. "Hey, everyone," I called out, "the Rishi's back!"

Of course I knew the good feeling was precarious as hell. So I drove without stopping, superstitiously. We'd lunched from our onboard supplies, as self-sufficient as a pair of astronauts. It took extra mental effort to acknowledge we were running out of gas.

"It's on E," Julie said.

"I know. I just want to get there."

"We won't if we run out."

"I know. I just don't want to take the time to stop."

Finally I capitulated right into a brand new Shell station in Alma, Kansas. Each pump was a command center with its key pad and printer and card swipe and intercom and menu of fuels. You half-expected an ICBM to rise from behind the mini-mart when you finished punching buttons. I bought a two-foot-tall bottled water from a cooler with a seal so tight I thought the door was locked. Julie took over the wheel.

As much as I hated stopping, I had to admit I badly needed the water. I drank the liters pretty fast. I had forgotten to drink for a while, so I filled up like a dry sponge. My stomach expanded, and each cell revived; previously beached nutrients and waste products began to wash through my system. I didn't bloat, just became full. But I didn't have to urinate. I remembered my last urination—dark yellow and feeble volume. It all made sense now.

"What do you want to bet I don't have to pee for two hundred miles?"

Julie yawned.

"I'm serious."

"You got dry," she said. "Now you're wet again."

"Is it making you wet, talking to me, your husband of five years?"

"No."

"Hmm."

"The next time I get wet," she said, "it'll be the Pacific Ocean that does it."

"All right, you're on. We'll wash in the Pacific."

"Not until then."

"Deal."

The sense of adventure soared right through the moonroof. We chased the sun. We ran out of crackers. Two hours later, I had to take a piss. Not badly, but definitely.

"Can we stop at the next rest area? I have to take a leak."

"Can you wait till we stop for dinner?"

"When's that?"

"Another hour."

Julie was codependent in wonderful and unpredictable ways. She furthered my urine-holding marathons as if she were the mouthpiece of an aspect of my psyche. This was in stark contrast to my counselor, who told me that holding my urine was related to a complex of feelings having to do with my father's death, just six months ago, from prostate cancer. "You're holding your urine because he never held *you*," Ron had explained.

"How many credit cards do we have to work with?" I asked, to take my mind off my bladder.

"We've got maybe fifteen thousand in credit."

"God, we've got potential."

We were getting into the really flat part of Kansas. I saw an exit for the town of Voda. Wheat grew like a brush haircut on both sides of the interstate, and purple thunderclouds towered ahead like the spume of a volcanic eruption. You could see why Bob Dole had had this state in his back pocket for all those years.

Julie said, "I've been thinking more spiritually lately."

I froze. Careful now, I thought. Don't set her off.

"That's interesting," I said cautiously. "Maybe we can get our heads read in California. I bet they have good phrenologists out there."

"I'm sort of afraid of that."

"You've got a great head."

"No, I mean I believe in it. I'm afraid to find out. I never took an IQ test. I don't want to know stuff like that. I like to think I've got potential."

"You've got a lot of potential."

"You say that like your mom."

"I mean it like my mom," I said. "And you're responding like my mom would respond if someone behaved like my mom to her. I've noticed that. You can neutralize her by behaving toward her in the same solicitous, encouraging way she behaves toward you. Just ask her how she's doing, get real interested in her, and she pretty much shuts down."

"That reminds me of a woman at work," Julie said. "She used to say 'hi' to me in exactly the same way I said 'hi' to her. The same intonation, everything. I'd say, 'How's it going?' and she'd say it right back to me: 'How's it going?' It really upset me."

"It's a weird thing," I said, "the way people talk." I was desperate to get her to stop talking about work, which had been the subject of far too many monologue meltdowns that spiraled wildly off-topic, leading to such non sequiturs as she wasn't sure she wanted to be married to me, or that she was thinking of suicide—not as something she would definitely do but as something she had "put on the table."

Grape-sized drops burst against the windshield. Julie's hands tightened on the steering wheel as the rain abruptly picked up, falling in spears that struck up white sparks when they hit the pavement. All at once the sky had become a lowering uniform gray, and the air was turning into water and tiny bits of hail and lightning. The windshield wipers were useless. It sounded like a dump truck was unloading gravel on the roof of the car.

"Easy," I said. Traffic all around us was slowing. Julie gave no sign that she was freaked out, but I knew she was. Her father was an exploder and she had perfected the display of calm in the face of the random release of dangerous forces.

From out of nowhere, a truck passed us on the right, like a leviathan suddenly breaching, so close its running lights faintly illuminated the interior of our car. "Holy moley!" I said.

The rain fell harder. It was absurd, as if we were in a car wash. No visibility whatsoever. Julie came to a complete stop in the left lane.

"Get over, get over!" I yelled, bracing for a rear-end collision.

I always ended up yelling at her. Never once have I wanted to yell at her, but I have yelled at her many times. She started crying silently, hands high on the wheel, elbows locked, maybe already taking the impact I was bracing for.

I might have bailed out of the car if I didn't fear the traffic in the right lane. Really, though, who knew what lane we were in?

During a few long minutes it seemed as though it would rain like this forever, then suddenly it was low tide. A half-dozen cars appeared ahead, pulled over to the shoulder or parked under an overpass. Julie started the car forward, and in another two minutes great, straight-from-the-brow-of-God shafts of sunlight broke through the deteriorating clouds.

We exited onto a street of franchises and found a Ponderosa.

"Good job, Champ," I said in the parking lot, and I patted her shoulder. She seemed to neither accept nor reject this.

We ordered our steaks and sat in a tall booth with glossy varnished wood planks rising on three sides of us. We had our plastic trays and our numbered pyramids indicating cut of meat. The place was alarmingly underlit.

"I wish you wouldn't yell at me," she said.

"I know. I panicked. I'm sorry."

We were both hungry and knew that it was up to one of us to go to the bathroom so that the food would come, because that's the best way to get food to show at your table. It should have been me, of course, but I was pleasantly surprised that something as exciting and suggestive as a massive downpour had not brought my need to urinate to a crisis. I had the satisfaction of a weight lifter who was bench-pressing four hundred pounds while remembering how once he could do only ninety.

"Why don't you go?" she said, which I took as a form of forgiveness.

"I'm OK now. I'd like to drink some more." I had a tall, blue-tinted plastic glass of ice water on my tray. It tasted fantastic, perfectly cold and pure. "I'd like to make sure my urine will run clear."

She put the strap of her purse over her shoulder and was about to slide out of the booth when the food arrived. We both had rib-eye steaks. We reached for the A-1 simultaneously.

"It's yours," I said.

"Thanks."

Ponderosa steak takes forever to chew. I had forgotten that again.

"I'm tired," she said. She had barely made a dent in her steak, which was as rectangular as Kansas itself. "I'm depressed," she said. Tears welled up in her eyes.

It no longer affected me that much to see her cry. At first, it really freaked me out. Now, though, I told myself that there was nothing I could do about it. I'd given every motivational speech I could think of, promised ridiculous levels of emotional support. But now I stayed on shore when she got depressed. And if I was depressed, I got back on land in a hurry, so that both of us would not be in the water at the same time.

"What's up?" I asked. It took a lot of restraint not to say, "I told you you shouldn't have quit your job. I told you that wasn't going to solve anything." Now that she'd given the corporate world the boot, she wanted to study sociology or psychology, or maybe anthropology. These plus history and we had all the useless disciplines covered. The unspoken idea was that I'd been hiding in school all this time, and now it was her turn to hide while I got a job. The only problem was that I'd had nothing but false starts with my dissertation. My area was the U.S. Civil War, and it had been written to death. I'd gone from the black northern regiments, to infighting in the Lincoln White House, to the first two years of Reconstruction, flailing against the giants in my field with my wet-noodle, fifth-grader theories. She was counting on my success at the very

moment the exact shape of my failure, which I had been conjuring
for decades, was finally coming into view. I was superpissed at her
counselor, who, after months of hashing this out, apparently had
advised, "Just go for it." Did she need to pay a trained professional
for this crap? Not to mention how much more we would be paying
for our mental health (including Julie's obviously insufficient Paxil
doses) when the COBRA benefits from her health plan ran out in a
few months.

"I don't know. I'm just tired. Let's not go much further."

"Do you want to sleep in the car? You might be tempted by a
motel shower."

"I won't be," she said.

"Coming right up. I'll drive. You rest. First decent place, we'll
start running up those credit cards."

An hour and a half later, we stopped at the Comfort Inn in Li-
mon, Colorado. I almost soaked my shorts writing our license plate
number on the registry card. I was anxious but really happy, too.
No matter when or where I finally pissed, it would be a clear and
powerful stream.

The hallway to our room went on forever. I knew what it was like
to drive a team of sled dogs across icy tundra, bringing a diphthe-
ria vaccine to an isolated, epidemic-stricken Alaskan town. It was
that good. When I finally let it go, it was an inhumanly powerful
stream: the vertical spray from the slit in the glans was an inch tall,
then it miraculously flattened out for a quarter inch before twisting
into a thick rope of urine that hardly frayed as it descended. Not as
clear as I had hoped for, but this was no tinkle: it was a thunderous
discharge that visibly raised the water level in the bowl. My groin

tingled with a sort of postorgasmic warmth. I flushed, brushed my teeth, and, otherwise unwashed, entered the main room.

She was on her back on the bed, fully clothed, laid out like a corpse. She knew I liked to undress her. While I did, she just lay there; she didn't help. It was a special thing we did, when we had time. It's a lot of work undressing someone who won't help, like undressing and dressing a corpse, I guess, which is not a one-man job.

It took me about fifteen minutes to get her down to her panties and into her pajama suit. Her eyes filled again and she sniffled. I pulled the covers out from under her, like the old tablecloth trick in slow motion, got in next to her. And prayed she wouldn't start talking.

There was no hope for sex. She had pretty much lost interest.

"You want to watch something to go to sleep by?" I asked.

"Whatever you want," she said.

We saw the last half of *The Creature from the Black Lagoon* on the USA channel. How I loved that awful scene when he takes Kay over the side of the boat and swims her down to his underwater cave—of course, I was rooting for the Creature, that huge man-fish!

"Why do you think David Reed won't marry Kay?" Julie asked me.

"Because deep down he's a bastard, except the movie can't show it. Actually, now that they've escaped the Creature, he probably will marry her."

"So it's like he has to conquer his inner creature to marry her? Is that the way guys are?"

Maybe if she had said this with a teasing smile, I might have

come back with something, but she said it with the seriousness
that warned me a three-hour discussion could ensue. So I shrugged.
"Let's hit it," I said.

Lights out. A quick kiss good night. We told each other we loved
each other and rolled to our respective sides of the bed. We love
each otter, I said to myself. Instead of closing my eyes and counting otters swimming by, I made the mistake of looking around the
strange, darkened room—a surefire invitation to insomnia. I decided to let it come. The best way to have insomnia is to relax. Accept those hours you can't sleep between midnight and 6:00 AM as
quiet time, time to get some rest.

My mind woke up. I thought of dear old Dad, dead at sixty-two.
Father's Day was five days away, and I'd been savoring not having
to buy him anything. This relief was the clearest emotion I had felt
since his death. When we got home after his funeral, I'd taken off
my suit jacket and started unknotting my tie when I remembered
how, in the year after I graduated from clip-ons, I always had to ask
him to tie my ties for me. It seemed as if I were about to cry and so I
tried to help it along. I kept making a noise like "Cheese!" or "Jeez!" I
whimpered, but I couldn't convince myself I was crying. Then Julie
came in the bedroom. "Bless you," she said.

The sad thing was that, after his diagnosis but before he was hos-
pitalized, it looked like something might happen between us. Tom
and Margaret, my brother and sister, lived out of town with their
spouses and kids, so when the family closed ranks around my father during his illness it was me and Julie and Mom. We'd go over
there for Sunday dinner. Mom and Julie would be cooking; the football game would be on to keep me company; and Dad would be at
his PC in the corner of the living room, writing yet another letter

to the editors of *Sports Illustrated.* Once he looked up just before I sat down on the couch and asked, "How's the dissertation coming?" I said, "Pretty good." And he said, "Writing's a bitch, ain't it?" and went back to his letter. I saw a printout of one of his drafts, and even in this you could see desperate emotion trying to peek through. Apparently he had reached the metalevel in his correspondence, the problem being that not one of his letters had ever been published or answered. "Surely," this single-spaced broadside insinuated midway through the second page, "the professional writers at *SI* are not intimidated by an amateur like myself. Yet what am I to make of your silence?"

Then I remembered the beautiful duet the Creature swims with unsuspecting Kay, frolicking beneath her instead of killing her, springing his amphibious boner in the weeds as she does her solo underwater ballet, and I thought about the woman at the front desk. She was all alone and sort of attractive. I could not easily take her in while hopping from foot to foot during check-in, but now I thought of her brisk way of speaking, the bright directness of her eyes, the extra something in her body movements as if she thought she were sexy. There was an indoor pool down the hall from the desk. I imagined it as a bed she took people to.

I tried to put her out of my mind, but fantasies crowded in relentlessly. My wife was safely asleep. I worked through the scenario: I had insomnia, I went for a walk. I didn't think beyond getting a better look at her, flirting with her. I would hang around her as long as she would let me. Not with adulterous intent, but just to enjoy being by her. I would be shameless in my lingering.

I had never cheated on my wife, and it was all but certain that this clerk would snub me, but I was under a strange compulsion.

Sometimes when I'm anxious or depressed, any old compulsion can grab me by the nose and lead me where it will. I got out of bed and put on my bathing suit and a T-shirt, took one of the big white rough-textured towels from the bathroom, and headed for the front desk.

She was there, reading *USA Today*. She looked up and smiled when I approached, tucked her straight brown hair behind her right ear. It was about 1:15 AM.

She didn't ask, "Can I help you?" She just looked at me.

I almost lost my nerve, but when I spoke my voice came out controlled and normal sounding.

"I know it's late, but I was wondering—I'm on a strict exercise program—it's a heart problem—and I need a certain amount of cardiovascular exercise and I've been sitting in the car all day—"

"You want to use the pool?" She stashed her newspaper, stood up, and leaned on the counter, with her elbows stretched forward, not a professional posture in the least.

"I do," I said.

"I suppose you probably know it's closed." She stepped back, pulled off a sticky note from somewhere under the counter, crumpled it, and threw it in a short rectangular trash can.

"You know I was curious as to why it might be closed. I mean, it's not like there's a lifeguard on duty during the day and not at night."

"It could get noisy," she said, more a suggestion than a definitive statement. She was young, maybe still in college.

"I wouldn't want to jeopardize your career," I said.

She hissed dismissively, as only a teenager would, but her whole shtick, it seemed, was to act mature and nonchalant. "I'm just doing this on summer vacation."

"Ah," I said. "Where're you going to school?"

"Colorado College. But I'm going on study abroad this fall. I'm going to Kenya."

"Very cool," I said.

"I suppose you can swim for a half hour."

"You can lock me in and turn out the light. I won't make much noise. Only when I surface. When I surface, I spout." I forcefully expelled air out of the corner of my mouth.

She laughed, briefly but involuntarily. "I bet you do," she said. She put a cardboard sign on the desk: "Back in five minutes." Then she went to the back of her little area and opened a door. I could hear that same door opening around the corner.

I followed her down the hallway, the air growing slightly more humid and chlorinated as we walked. Her arms and legs swung energetically, one hand clutching a ring of keys. She was short and hippy; her best feature was her pretty, yearning, inquiring face. Ahead, the pool room looked dark.

She turned the bolt in the glass door and held it open. "Here you go," she said.

I thought everything depended on getting her to enter the pool area with me.

"What does your boyfriend think of you going to Kenya?" I asked lamely.

"Don't have one, right now," she said, pushing her chest forward a bit, defiance overriding embarrassment. She moved to keep the door open with her back.

She wasn't especially attractive, but her sexual confidence was getting to me. I could see her screwing some Kenyan in a clay hut after plantains and goat meat. She was the type of woman who would ask her boyfriend, "Do you want to fuck now?"

"Are you a risk taker?" I said. I couldn't dwell on how creepy and predatory this made me sound. The compulsion was talking.

"Depends."

"You seem like one," I said. My mouth was going dry, and I was getting hard. But the whole situation had the feeling of a game, like holding your breath underwater as long as you can.

"Does your wife think *you're* a risk taker?"

"We're divorcing," I said, so easily it scared me. "It's over."

"Don't bullshit me," she said. She moved her shoulders back, slouching against the door. The word "bullshit" was the sword and shield of her deep experience of life.

But she didn't leave. I reached for her hand. She let me take it. "OK, I won't," I said, and I bent down and kissed her.

She went right for my crotch, as quickly as a martial artist, and squeezed me perfectly, and I knew I was doomed.

We pulled a reclining lounge chair into a shadowy corner, by a large potted tree, out of view of anyone coming down the hall, well away from the parking lot light, which shone through two walls of windows.

She wouldn't have intercourse without a condom, so we lay on the stretchy vinyl slats of the lounger, with her skirt up and my swim shorts down. We worked each other expertly. It didn't take long for either of us.

"Thanks," she said jauntily, and she stood.

"Yeah, thanks," I said. Remorse was already flooding in, but I was still tingling from how intense the sex was.

She tucked in her blouse and straightened her skirt. "Have a good swim," she said, and she laughed.

"I will," I said.

"Let yourself out," she added.

When she had left, I eased myself into the warm, kidney-shaped pool, and waded slowly through the shallow end, Creature style, with my arms in front of me as if I were carrying a limp woman, unconscious with fear. This was a sign of the idiotic zaniness I fell into whenever my life looked like a bucket of shit. I tried to stem the rising sense of gloom and self-disgust with the notion that we didn't actually have intercourse, so maybe I hadn't committed adultery—what grad student jokers a hundred years from now will call "The Clinton Doctrine." But that didn't work. I told myself I would be nicer to Julie, not in a conspicuous way, but in a good and steady way. Really, this was so wrong that I was sure it would bring me to my senses.

I swam down deep into the pool, finding the warm jets, recoiling from the underwater lights, as the Creature would. I wondered if my pops had ever stepped out on my mom. There was a woman at church who always made him rub his hands together excitedly when they exchanged small talk on the steps, but who knew. Then I realized I had violated our pledge not to bathe until we reached the Pacific Ocean. I needed to leave the pool immediately, dry off, and then perform activities that would somehow recoat myself with a day's worth of grime. I could transfer my feelings of remorse to this act, so that if Julie got suspicious, I would confess to swimming in the pool, and it would clear the air.

After swimming until all signs of the clerk had been washed away, I emerged from the pool determined to cover myself with a more righteous slime. The best thing would be to get junk food from a machine and then work that through my pores with a long walk or a short jog. But I didn't want to risk going back to the room to get my wallet. I fished in the pockets of my swimming suit and almost burst into tears when I found three soaked dollars folded up, which I'd stuffed in there almost a year ago when we were visiting our pals in Boston and had gone swimming at Singing Beach. The bills were still good, but damp.

I headed to the desk. The clerk was back to reading *USA Today*, as if nothing had happened. "Back so soon. How's your heart?"

"Better," I said blandly. "Could I trade you these wet dollar bills for some dry ones? For the candy machines." I released a huge amount of air after I said this. I hadn't known that I was holding in so much.

"You're diabetic, too?"

I was starting to hate her stupid aggressive confidence, so I just smiled.

She dug around in her purse and slapped three dry dollar bills on the counter. I climbed the back stairs to the second floor. As soon as I opened the heavy fire door, I heard talking. I rounded a corner and there were two people standing in a nook with gleaming vending machines—and the two people were Julie and a man in gym shorts and a T-shirt with a sailboat on it.

If my towel wasn't slung over my shoulder, I would have dropped it. As it was, I gave a real start. Julie drank it in calmly. She was back in her blue jeans and T-shirt. I remembered painstakingly undressing her.

"There you are," she said. "Burt, this is my husband, Mike. Mike, Burt."

"How do you do?" I said, and I stretched out my hand, which Burt shook, his grip surprisingly weak and cold.

"Burt sells software," Julie said.

"Oh, I bet that's good," I said.

"Let me just get some ice here," Burt said. He picked up his little tan bucket and slid the door open and got right in there with the scoop.

"Burt's going to drink himself to sleep," Julie said. "I could use a drink myself."

"I heard it's not that good to drink yourself to sleep," I said. "The alcohol wakes you up later."

Burt had filled his bucket. "You people have a good night," he said, and he took off down the hall.

"You've been in the water," Julie said, with her arms crossed. "Why?"

"It was a mistake." I told myself the sick guilty look on my face would be for the swimming and she would never know. "What are you doing here?"

"Looking for you." Her voice broke. She looked at me steadily for a moment, then turned away, her arms still crossed. She shouldered open the fire door and headed up to our floor.

"It was a mistake," I said, following her into the stairwell.

She sat down on the steps, just high enough to look straight over my head at the cinderblock wall painted a wet-looking cream color.

"I just wanted to talk to someone," she said. Then she started to cry.

I put out my right hand and touched a glass case that had about
a hundred yards of fire hose inside. My thundering urination now
seemed like a happy event from someone else's life. I blinked hard
and the chlorine from the pool stung my eyes. But I knew I wouldn't
cry. I knew that no matter what she said or did, I would not cry, that
only a direct blow to me personally could make me cry. I could not
cry for anyone else, at all, ever.

"Is an alcoholic software salesman in a sailboat T-shirt really the
kind of man you want to talk to?"

She hit her closed fist against her forehead and mouthed, "Yes,"
and now she was crying hard.

"Go ahead and talk to me," I said, though it took all of my effort.

She didn't say anything for a while. I sat down on the bottom
step and looked up at her. For a minute, I felt relief. It was as if I had
called her bluff and what I was afraid of— her unspooling a long
anxious monologue that would surely drag me down with her—
was not going to happen.

She gradually gathered herself. It took so long that I had plenty
of time to get bored and wonder why I was such a shit for not figur-
ing out how to support her, for not even being moved that much by
her crying.

"Why do you study history?" she finally said.

"Why do I study history? I have no idea."

"Are you interested in civil wars?"

The sincerity of her question broke my heart. She had no clue
what a flaming rickety shithouse grad school was. "I don't give a
hoot about any of it," I said. "Except I don't want to fail."

The truth is supposed to set you free, but she just blinked at it.

Her eyes were now permanently looking over my head. She wiped tears with the back of her hand.

I thought I should embrace her, so I moved to do this. She would like it and it might end the talking. We stood up in the stairwell and we hugged each other hard. She cried behind my back.

"It's OK," I said.

"It's not OK."

"Well, maybe it is."

* * *

The next day was sunny and beautiful. It was the exact opposite of the weather on the day Dad gave it up: a foot of wet snow, and every nurse and doctor on the ward nervously eyeing the tiny, incessant flakes, talking about it at their stations, while Dad performed his uneventful slide into oblivion.

When I got up, Julie wasn't in bed. She was probably in a coffee shop somewhere, or in the Mac's across the street, writing in her journal.

I went into the bathroom to take a piss, resetting the meter, so to speak, before deciding on the day's urine management strategy. When I turned on the light, I nearly jumped out of my skin. She was sitting on the toilet in the dark.

"Are you all right?" I asked.

"No," she said.

"Do you still want to go to California?" This seemed to me the operative question at the moment, but she started crying again.

She didn't say anything else. Possibly, she had given up on talking to me, and I was relieved about this while also feeling guilty. But

I thought that—I don't know what I thought. It was as if she sensed what I had done and it was making her cry.

"Let's get some breakfast," I said.

She didn't object to this. Neither of us knew what to do; we could only do things that we had done every day up to this point. I realized that my pledge to behave better toward her might finally resolve into this: behaving the same way I always behaved.

I took us to the Mac's drive-thru, as if I were escorting a prisoner between jails and didn't want to give her a chance to escape. We got a pair of Egg McMuffins and I ordered two hash browns instead of one. Then I changed my order to four hash browns, because I loved their hot greasy salty potato taste, somewhat crispy on the outside and moist and slimy on the inside.

I picked up the food and swerved into a parking space. I opened my Egg McMuffin between my thighs, punched a straw through the foil of my OJ and stuck it between the emergency brake and my bucket seat, then stacked my hash browns on the dashboard so the group could preserve their warmth, wedged between the box of Kleenex and the control panel hump.

Julie let the bag rest on her lap. I took us into traffic.

"Are you not hungry?" I asked, already into my second hash brown. I had to eat my hash browns at a certain temperature.

She unwrapped her Egg McMuffin. I drove and noticed she had gone no further. As soon as my attention to her ran out, her motor ran down. I ate at a ridiculously fast pace, scarfing a bite of Egg McMuffin, swallowing half a hash brown, sucking on my OJ.

Up ahead, the Rockies stood like a gray-blue wall on the horizon. There was no way our little Honda could climb them. We would charge up but then roll back down, like a marble settling in a trough. Julie held her Egg McMuffin unbitten in her hand, as if stymied by this impossibility.

"Go ahead and eat," I said. "No one has ever felt right on an empty stomach."

She took a bite.

About five miles later, she said, "I don't feel well," with her mouth still full. "Pull over. Please."

She was going to vomit, so I pulled over.

When I came to a stop, she sat for about ten seconds before she reached over and undid her seat belt. The car beeped about an unsecured passenger but soon gave up. She was still holding her Egg McMuffin. It took a mighty act of self-restraint not to yell, "If you're going to puke, get out of the car!" Instead I said, "Are you all right?" but with a tone that actually had the effect of "If you're going to puke, get out of the car!"

Finally, she got out, and stood, swaying. Before I could ask what she was doing, she slammed the door. Fine, I thought, and turned off the engine. The slam was a slap in the face, but I was always relieved by distancing gestures, especially those I didn't need to perform myself. I punched on the hazard flashers and settled in.

Through the window, I could see only her torso. Just then her mouthful of food fell down the front of her shirt. This was worse than vomiting, and the explanation could not be a happy one. She was outside our car like an astronaut on a space walk, and I had to stay in the car and man the ship or we both risked drifting away. She walked forward, slowly, and I saw that she must have dropped her Egg McMuffin.

In the end, after the radiation seeds failed, my father got weepy, or, I should say, weepier. For someone who often treated other peo-

ple as if they didn't have emotions, who spoke to his kids as if we
were employees, he was often moved to tears. He got "choked up,"
as he would say, at certain predictable family events—at holidays,
when his kids got married, and in the days leading up to his retire-
ment, which he saw as one of the more momentous days in human history. Before his diagnosis, of course. His choking up always
struck me as self-centered and sentimental, but it could be that I
just liked to imagine the worst about him.

When I wonder if I'm being too hard on him, I remember what
he said to my brother Tom a few years ago, when we were on a fish-
ing trip on Lake of the Woods in Minnesota. We were getting ready
to go out one morning—stuffing our coolers with sandwiches and
Cokes, gathering our tackle, slipping windbreakers over sweat-
shirts—when Tom said something to himself about a towel he was
looking for. "A towel?" Dad said peevishly, taking offense, I think,
because as Trip Manager he had not envisioned people needing
towels. "What do you need a towel for?" Tom said something about
drying the dew off the boat seats, wiping his hands after putting
a leech on a hook. When Pops got incredulous, Tom asked, "Well,
what do you wipe your hands on?" "On you!" our father crowed. "I
wipe my hands on you!"

This was before we had gotten any fish, and the weather was bad,
and Dad was worried about whether the trip would be everything
he wanted it to be. I knew that at a certain level what he said was
a displacement of some other, maybe legitimate, anger or anxiety. And maybe wiping off your crap on other people—or just not
dealing with something straight, for what it is instead of what you
bring to it—was an inescapable rule of life. I probably did it to Julie
in a hundred different ways without realizing it. I probably did it to
myself, too. I couldn't face even my small man's problems directly;

I had to distract, displace, transfer: play games with my bladder, diddle a hotel clerk, let *other* become *otter* become *creature*, instead of doing—what? Damn, I sucked as a historian.

Julie drifted around the right headlight and moved across the front of the car, her left hand trailing across the Honda's low hood. A stream of cars passed by. It seemed as if I were just coming upon her while driving along in my life. I was going to hit her, kill her, but I wasn't moving. We were in the breakdown lane, but her eyes were lowered, as if she were imagining something elsewhere.

Then she got on her knees in front of the car, and lay down, out of sight. I watched to see if she would get up. I listened for sounds of her tampering with the car. But she wasn't checking the struts; she was just there, maybe composing a loony tune or swimming down to inspect funk and mental illness.

It occurred to me that it was time to tiptoe out of this marriage. I didn't doubt that in some deep way we belonged together, but what if that bond was based on a mutual propensity for failure and looniness? Call it self-defense: I wasn't going to get dragged down with her. I was ready to let her go, crossing the old Rubicon of divorce by just sitting there, which was my way, a sitting there that said "distance, distance, distance." And the longer I sat there, the clearer this message would be. But I couldn't silence a line of backtalk: "You're just the sort of bastard who would abandon his depressed wife on interstate gravel. You're the type of small philandering man everyone hates!"

I got out of the car and went around to the front. She was lying face down, with one cheek resting on the pavement and both arms thrown over her head, as if she had fallen over in the middle of a jumping jack.

"Hey, what's up with that?" I said. I hated this expression, but that didn't stop me from using it. "What you're doing." At moments of great emotional intensity, I speak with extreme clumsiness: my way of crying, I guess.

She didn't say anything, so I crouched down by her face.

"Hey there," I tried.

"I'm so tired," she said. Her eyes were closed. "I was coming over to drive," she added, in a voice that was crumbling like a sand castle in front of a wave.

"You're scaring me," I said. "Please don't, Sweetie, do that."

"You hate me," she said, and tears ran out of her closed eyes. "You wish I would go away."

"No, not true," I said idiotically. "Don't you know that I love you a lot?"

"No—I don't know."

"Please, come on, get up. This is not safe to do. You start acting out this stuff and then you probably turn out really doing it."

"I can't."

"You can, for sure."

"I can't. Can't move. No more."

"Julie," I said. "Hey." But she lay there.

I slid my arms under her and picked her up. It was like maneuvering her when I was undressing her on the bed, which now struck me as a completely morbid practice. I got her in my arms and lifted her. She was lighter than I ever remembered. She kept her eyes closed hard against what I was doing.

"You know why you don't know that I love you?" I said. "Because a lot of times I'm a real jackass. I'm going to get me a T-shirt with 'Here comes shithead' printed on it."

Her eyes opened and she looked at me disbelievingly. Maybe my self-loathing was not what she needed at the moment. But I couldn't even let the question of whether I really loved her, of whether I was at all good for her, happen. The fact was, I *had* to love her, to be sane, to have an endurable idea of myself. "I still love you a lot," I said.

She stared at me, still crying fitfully. I thought, Who could hear those words and not want to believe everything they could possibly mean?

Beach

He always try to change but he cannot because he fit his passion on a star. And hover there.

Me I turn milk in his arms and then flow.

Shame on us.

He so strong. He smell strong certainly. He say he cool, but I pretty sure he done something the other night. Somebody got they face shot off.

The ocean have a motion. It come at us. The sky have a color that the water wants to know. Look down this beach. They be crabs in them sandy holes. They run to they holes when we come along—all different sizes. Spider size. Crab size. He like that. Remind him of walking down North King Street. People hide in they holes as he go by. He a big man.

"Mean streets," I say. "What they mean?"

"They mean," he say, "the presence of you, that is, pure love, pure love."

"Go and be dried. Take up your towel and walk. You have ruint the ocean like as you ruint the man you killt."

"Oh, come on. Who killed nobody? Heh, heh."

We been swimming. We been underwater. Say to myself: You go underwater to change yoself. You like to think you be different when you come back up. But the water don't know how to make you different. Then the sun dry you off. But it don't know neither. Now I walk where the sand be wet under sliding water. Yearning wave. But what can a wave know? Maybe the wave say there be deeper sand. Firm in its heart. Untoucht. Unmelt.

"Come here," he say, with his voice in his head. Come out his eye. More than mouth. Come out his nose, ear. Come out like a loud-speaker.

"Why? You gon kill me I don't?"

"Maybe I will. Heh, heh."

"You threaten me at yo own risk."

"Why you gettin on me?"

"You act like you got privileges."

"Don't I?"

"I don't love nobody. So nobody know me like you want to know me."

"I already 'know you' know you."

"How you *know me* know me? What the fuck's your problem? You already ruin the ocean, why you wan ruin me?"

"Oh, that's cold. That's real cold."

"Uh-huh."

"Meant to say I know you, only because I be thinkin about you so much."

"Is that why you be drooling all the time?"

"Damn, you cold."

Say to myself: Hang the ocean out to dry and what do you get? This man. *This* man. He would kill over money. He live off the street—make a thousand dollars a day *bein* the man. He's some in-visible hand man driving people crazy with his supply and demand. Everybody be comin to him, but he don't do it hisself. So he say. But he touch my ass now. What good his word? Who he? Who he?

"Shot a man with a gun. You scare me."

He laugh. Maybe he proud. Maybe he acting like I'm joking.

"You think I like being with a killer? That's a whole nother level."

He smile something you don't ever want to see. Smile took off happy enough til over some cliff it got lost. Now it all messed up like a monster got a grip on his face.

"You think you special," he say. "You think you God. I broken. I know it. You cain't be telling me I'm not. I broken. Ain't gonna put *me* in the world. I cain't even see the world."

There be a beach dog rub his back into a dead seagull. There be a beach dog, all nasty, perplexed by the dead bird. Crazy dog. I ain't against this man, but why I like rubbing up against the dead my own self? He like a dead man. That's what you be if you kill somebody. That's how it come around. And it always do. Tell me he done nothing when I hear the trash cans rattle at night and he reach for the drawer of his nightstand. And them two dogs take it up and it go back and forth and he sit up and wait. They chase. They know. Dog know. Dog chase. And then I know I got to get up and get on home; my mama be worrying. My daddy be out driving his cab, one eye peeled for me at all times. And every second I don't go I feel more feeble. Not built by my own hands. This a lot like dying. Itself.

He goin on about the world.

"I cain't see the world. I ain't in the world."

He can tell it don't move me.

"Woman, I *buy* you things."

"You got money to burn. It don't mean nothing to you."

"Aw, you so young."

"I so young."

"You stupid."

"*You* just fucked up."

"Don't tell *me* when I fucked up."

"Whoa. What I make you remember? What yo mama say? What happened the day you was born? Did God come and give it up or didn't he like you?"

"You crazy."

"I crazy."

"You so young I shouldn't waste my time wi' chew."

"You shouldn't waste your time with nobody. Where this beach? Why you bring me here?"

"I want you to love me, baby. I cain't take you with me, you don't love me."

"I got to be in schoo next week. I got to be in schoo."

"Naw," he say. "We got to go to New Orleans."

"They after you. You gonna be killt in a flaming house. You gonna die in some restaurant. You maybe Clyde. I ain't no Bonnie."

"Huh."

He stop and bend over to the sand. He pick up a handful of sand. He sift it. "I tell you something," he say. "I feel good now. I do. Right now I think I could stop it. Somewheres out of the neighborhood. Get someplace else."

"And leave your mama and your brothers and sisters—and me?"

"I said I'm taking you with me. What else can I do?"

"That's a good question. I told you I ain't going."

"Fuck you, bitch."

"Fuck you, motherfucker."

"Whoa, bitch, watch yoself. All the shit I bought for you—I take you everywhere. What you want?"

"What nobody know."

"Fuck that shit!"

"What *no*body know."

"Shut up, bitch!"

"What nobody *know*!"

Now he don't hit me. Something leave him, like a demon or maybe his own self. His face get all retarded, but his body be a humming wire. He holding himself just stretched, not broke.

I still be waiting for his hard hand. But he don't hit me. He control hisself, like some kind of wise man. I surprised. Tilted head think a thought: What can he know? What his passion for now and to be trying?

He be breathing fast. His eyes be wet and stupid.

Makes a feeling in me: Maybe should I take his hand. Maybe should I hold it to my face.

Don't nobody try this.

This is his head—bruised, soft-seeming, like a peach somebody rolled down stairs. He talks through his nose, has a deviated septum. Plus his nose was once busted and never healed right, plus he wouldn't be good at talking with a perfect nose. There's something wrong with his mouth. Stephen Wendell Osborne.

Stephen loves women, their feet especially. He likes acute arches, the second toe longer than the big toe; he likes narrow but not bony. Shoes drive him crazy. The putting on and the taking off of nylons drive him crazy. He's not well. The fetish is a black hole for attention he's supposed to spend on lawyering. Red in the face, hot under the eyes, smelling of his own saliva, he can hardly draft his memos, do his research, depose his witnesses—all on account of the fetish and his tireless trolling of the World Wide Web for images of feet and their accouterments. ToeJob.com. Footlover.com. Footfetish.com. He plunks down for the monthly membership, downloads the videos, but soon they wear off after repeated viewings and he must find fresh (or, occasionally, dirty) feet. He takes incredible risks to bring himself off while encountering feet sites. He's brought himself off in his office (bought a coat tree to block the view from the hallway) as well as in many Cook County public and law school libraries.

Stephen goes to court one day for a discovery conference in the matter of *Borgan v. Cessna Corp. et al.* He gets agitated upon spying the feet of Sally Cunningham, the skinny, sharp-nosed, raven-haired attorney over there at the plaintiff's table. She slips a deeply arched length of nylon-clad foot out of her pump and scratches the back of her opposite calf with it. Slack-jawed and staring, Stephen makes a loud, involuntary noise.

The judge is not insensible. He requests a consult with counsel in chambers. Stephen goes back there, and the judge yells at him, uses the phrase "my courtroom" a dozen times. Shame breaks into a running sweat on Stephen's face. He says "I understand, Your Honor" repeatedly. He feels his unusually small mouth getting rubbery and tight, hears his out-of-plumb nose give his words a peculiar, sonorous quality. "I understand, Your Honor. I understand."

They return to the courtroom, where Cunningham pages through her legal pad, absently bouncing her crossed leg. Her pump, off the heel again, dangles from her toes and sways with her bouncing. Stephen takes his seat, cross-eyed with renewed desire. Cunningham rises, quickly and cogently proposes some limits to the discovery process that will hamstring Stephen. He makes a brief incoherent reply. The judge rules for the plaintiff and the lawyers quickly leave the courtroom.

Stephen is so chastened and demoralized that he doesn't even stalk Cunningham back to her office from a discreet distance, as he might otherwise do. Instead, he proceeds directly down La Salle Street to the Harris Bank building and his lair on the twenty-sixth floor, where he licks his wounds surrounded by cherry wood and dark red leather furnishings. He would like to open his web browser and have a consolatory bout of foot ogling, but he knows this is likely to cash out his afternoon and culminate in a high-risk ejaculation. With a Herculean effort, he turns to the window and prays for strength to the tall stone angels on the Board of Trade building setbacks.

Please, he silently prays, *let me focus all of my energies on aviation litigation.*

Stephen specializes in defending insurance companies in your weekend Cessna crash, your crop-dusting fiasco, your commercial airliner dropping from the sky just after takeoff. Coming up for partner next year, he manages a respectable two thousand billables per annum—including not a few bogus hours logged while actually on fetish patrol—but lately the managing partner has been riding him about settling too many cases too quickly. Stephen can't explain that the fetish sometimes prevents him from getting thoroughly prepped. Alternatively, he can't explain how he's wary of going to trial, even fully loaded, because during oral argument he might not be able to communicate his many good legal points because of his unusually small mouth and the out-of-plumb nose he is forced to talk through.

Please, he silently prays, *let me achieve an above-ankle relationship with an actual woman and thereby restrict my heretofore reckless and time-consuming sex practices to missionary intercourse with my beloved wife once or twice a week—and thereby leave sufficient time for aviation litigation!*

Instead of opening that foot browser, he finds himself scooting his chair across the carpet toward the cardboard box that contains his incipient *Borgan v. Cessna Corp. et al.* files.

Two days later, he deposes the paramedics in *Borgan*. The facts of the case are curious: While taxiing before takeoff, Richard Borgan runs his Cessna off the edge of the runway at DeKalb Municipal Airport. His girlfriend, Doris Chanilowski, is thrown from the plane and injured. Borgan asserts that the steering apparatus behaved convulsively before the accident. He sues on his own behalf to get compensation for a subtle but debilitating neck injury, plus the emotional distress of witnessing Doris prone and broken in the weeds on the side of the runway. (Doris is not a party to Borgan's suit, nor is she pursuing her own, which suggests she has been bribed or heavily manipulated by Borgan, probably because he knows that if she sues Cessna, Stephen will try to pin liability on Borgan's negligent and/or reckless steering.)

The first paramedic reveals that Doris was wearing a sundress with no underwear at the time of the accident, and that while examining her body for trauma he noticed what looked like a tampon string leading to her vagina, from which something yellow was bulging. The string turned out to be a cord connecting a series of small red and yellow plastic balls, which, the paramedic sheepishly narrates, he withdrew from her vagina at the scene. In a separate deposition, the second paramedic discloses that he discovered Borgan working under the steering column with a screwdriver.

On a hunch, Stephen asks the second paramedic, "And did you notice anything unusual about how Mr. Borgan was wearing his clothes?"

"Actually, yeah," the second paramedic says. "His pants were open."

"Meaning the fly was unbuttoned and unzipped?"

"That's right."

With these details in mind, Stephen approaches the deposition of Doris Chanilowski with an anticipatory frenzy. She turns out to be a big woman—easily 6'3", 210—but with great proportions and this huge energy about her. She's a receptionist at a large law firm around the corner from Stephen's office, on Monroe, and wears the same kind of business suit his own secretary would wear. Stephen is duly smitten by the five neatly arrayed toes that protrude like tiny bunny rabbits from the great cast that ensheathes her massive but well-proportioned lower leg. (She insists she will not wear the gargantuan sock a friend knit for her from hideous royal-blue yarn.)

Under oath, Doris lies expertly about the convulsive activity of the steering apparatus, but Stephen gets her to acknowledge that, judging by where she ended up on the ground, she must have been hanging out the door of the plane when the accident happened.

"Richard likes that sort of thing," she says, to the chagrin of attorney Cunningham.

Pretty darn sure the accident was caused by sexual hijinks, Stephen uses a cordial postdeposition moment to make a date with Doris. (Violation of Illinois Rules of Professional Conduct, Rule 1.7.(b) re: conflict of interest.)

He has hopes and so makes reservations at The 95th, a restaurant on top of the Hancock, dark to facilitate the spectacular nighttime views. Her toes peek out from the cast the entire night. They drink a lot of wine. Doris opens up to him quickly and immensely, like an enormous parachute. She claims to be "religious as hell." She has God like a yo-yo on a string, has Jesus in a jar on the shelf.

"That right?"

"Oh yeah," says Doris. "I got the Virgin Mary vacuuming my Toyota." She hits a big fist on the table for emphasis, and they both crack up laughing.

Stephen is charmed by the sincere–mock religious pride of the huge but well-proportioned Doris. "Speaking of blessed ladies," he says, "you look better in a cast than any woman I've ever seen." (Over the years, Stephen has learned that the best fetish-related gambits are always the most direct—more quick rejections, sure, but more acceptances overall.) "It's amazing how erotic toes and plaster can be."

"You think so?" Doris belly laughs, inspiring Stephen to think of underground tunnels. She gathers herself, then smiles into his eyes.

Stephen slurs, "I hope you're not embarrassed about those beads. I admire a woman who knows what she wants."

Doris confides that she actually likes *storing* things in her vagina. Her greatest fantasy is airport security. All the air travelers put their keys in the plastic basket. She's holding her keys inside, wrapped in a sandwich baggie. She goes through, the thing beeps. She empties her pockets, the thing beeps. They administer the handheld wand. Guess where it goes off! All roads lead to a cavity search. "It's humiliating, but I love it," she says. "Weird, huh?"

"Whoa," Stephen says respectfully.

"Anything to do with airports or planes makes me horny," she admits.

"Speaking of horny," Stephen says, "let me touch your toes," which induces another great laugh from Doris. But she slouches just enough to extend her encased foot across their booth to rest in his crotch. The encased foot juts from under the white tablecloth, seemingly ownerless. Stephen suddenly understands why surgeons cover the rest of a patient's body while cutting into a particular area.

"Well!" Doris exclaims as Stephen presses his erect penis directly against her toes, under cover of napkin, but she doesn't withdraw her cast. Most likely, she senses the paralyzing downward pressure Stephen is exerting on the cast with his other hand—until he finishes and blots off her toes with the napkin.

He wants to know how he can return the favor. Doris denudes his right foot, draws it up her dress, pulls her panties aside, and gets to work.

Does anyone notice? The tablecloth hangs low; the place is not too crowded but busy enough. Their waiter is a tall, handsome young man with moussed dark hair who is apparently *on something* and disappears from the dining room for ten minutes at a time. Jazz standards from the piano player. High-class goings on.

After she comes, Doris throws a knife on the floor and drapes her napkin over it.

* * *

Things are developing well with *Borgan,* so Stephen isn't too upset about his negative progress in terms of reining in the old fetish. He calls Sally Cunningham to announce that his expert has confirmed likely postaccident tampering with the steering apparatus, all his witnesses are singing from the same songbook, this litigation is history. Cunningham best mount her contingency-fee scooter and chase other ambulances.

But Cunningham asks to see what he's got, and when they meet in the bar at a venerable steakhouse on Jackson, she's wearing a pantsuit and Gaultier high heels. Stephen can't see much when she's walking, but when she sits down in the captain's chair at the tall little round table, he knows her cuffs have risen like a pair of curtains.

Stephen dismounts from his tall chair and ducks below the table to retrieve papers from his briefcase. But her feet are so amazingly perfect and so wonderfully set off by her shoes—low cut, revealing deep toe cleavage—that he suspects Sally might have set *him* up. (Later, he will learn she's a ringer, a former foot model for Lord & Taylor to make extra cash during her hard-driving days at DePaul Law School.) He gazes while pretending to rummage. Cunningham slyly works the strap of one of her high heels against a rung on her chair. Her shoe drops off.

"Oops," she says.

On his knees, beneath the table, Stephen has a private, unfettered view of her pedicured foot. He whimpers at his instantaneous erection. After an embarrassing amount of time, he surfaces. He gamely goes through the motions of being a lawyer with the upper hand. Showing her the damning excerpts from his expert's report, he judges how much he has to work with by the way her lips purse as she reads. But Cunningham casually says that she has yet to hear from her own expert and flashes him a winning smile. He makes quick calculations based on a devastating combination: high sexual desire and low self-esteem. Given his nose and mouth, and the classiness and beauty of Cunningham's feet, Stephen despairs of becoming her legitimate lover.

"Can we make a deal?" he asks, his mouth tightening.

"A deal," she says, without inflection.

Stephen watches his considerable legal advantage get mowed down by the overwhelming inexorability of the fetish. "You know," he says, "you have the most beautiful feet I've ever seen."

As a result of his relatively long and efficacious service to the Cessna Corporation and its insurers, Stephen has independent settlement authority up to $100,000, so he offers Cunningham and her client $55,000 in exchange for two sessions with those feet. (Violation of Illinois Rules of Professional Conduct, Rule 1.7.(b) re: conflict of interest.) Cunningham counteroffers, and a horny and perspiring Stephen capitulates within minutes at $150,000, leaving for later the problem of bluffing this past in-house insurance company counsel.

This is all well and good, but it doesn't exactly represent progress away from the fetish. Their encounters turn out to be agreeable. She is playful and experienced, doesn't ridicule him at all—neither for his fetish nor for his nose and mouth. After their second session, he steels himself to attempt, at last, an above-ankle relationship with her. He calls and asks her out for a drink. The conversation starts nice enough but eventually she calls him a creep. She metaphorically chalks a portable circle around her person with a radius of five hundred yards. Denies Stephen access.

Stephen accepts her assessment of his creepiness. Full of fresh anxiety and self-loathing, he redoubles his trolling of the web. His grip on his work becomes increasingly tenuous. He briefly contemplates getting help from an experienced psychologist but cannot stand the shame of fessing up to his issue in such a context. Instead, he begins to leave the office in the middle of the day and takes the El up to his favorite porn emporium on Broadway, with its selection of movies, equipment, and magazines as well as a nest of viewing booths around an area where a young woman, using only a metal folding chair for a prop, gyrates in ways that are vaguely off-putting and ridiculous, until Stephen proffers a twenty if she would just pull up her damn chair and put her dirty toes against the tip slot.

One day, before hitting the booths, he catches out of the corner of his eye what looks to be Doris shopping the dildos. Stephen has always been afraid to risk any eye contact in porn emporiums, so he finds a strategic lookout where he can seem to peruse videos but get a good look at the woman, who actually is Doris.

He approaches and asks, "Can I help you?"

"Stephen?" she says. "What brings you here?"

"Unresolved emotional issues."

"From your childhood?"

"From all the time."

"I see," says Doris.

"It's just so pleasurable."

"Gosh, that's true," Doris says, and she laughs companionably. "Hey, look." She lifts up her sandaled right foot.

"Doris," he says weakly. Her foot is huge but perfectly proportioned; it makes him think of Michelangelo's *David.*

"Hold on, Stephen. I mean the cast is off. We're having a party to celebrate—with all that great settlement money."

"We, as in you and Richard."

"Hey, I'm a loyal girl," Doris says.

"No one said you weren't."

"Oh, I thought maybe you thought otherwise."

"No, I'm never fooled by those types of, you know, encounters."

"Things aren't that great. I'm not leaving him right now. I will soon, though."

"Why, though, if I can ask?"

"You can ask. He's jealous of these." She holds a large dildo that is molded from the real erect penis of a porn star; every vein and swelling and contour is absolutely lifelike, except it's made of a translucent cherry-red plastic that looks like hardened jelly. Gold glitter squares float frozen inside. It's a very appealing dildo, Stephen thinks.

"Can't say as I blame him."

"But really? He thinks I'm a deviant. He found a marble in me the other night. I forgot about it."

Stephen gives her a moment of empathetic silence. "But he can't be too mad, if he's having a party about the cast coming off."

"He thinks he's talked me out of it."

In her other hand is a package, which at first Stephen thinks contains a strap-on dildo but really it's something worn so that the small curving beige pseudocock is always inside the vagina. The product is called "Little John." Tag line: "Your secret lover."

"He doesn't know what happened between us?" Stephen asks.

"You know, once he asked me what I did to get you to settle the case. You didn't settle because of me, did you?"

Stephen grins idiotically.

"Why don't you come to the party?"

"Why not? I will."

* * *

Roger Frost, the managing partner, is well respected at the firm. He's clearly a man's man, a lawyer's lawyer, a commuter's commuter. He urinates with his hands on his hips, feet more than shoulder-width apart; plays racquetball like a headmaster paddling recalcitrant schoolchildren; consumes food and drink only as needed.

Here now comes Stephen to stand before Frost, who is wearing one of his signature starched white shirts and an impeccably knotted red tie flecked with tiny shapes.

"Why on earth did you settle that Borgan case?"

Stephen doesn't respond. Frost snickers and tosses the scathing audit of *Borgan v. Cessna Corp. et al.* onto his desk. "This is a heads-up," he says. "You're not likely to make partner next year. Nothing more's coming your way. Get your files ready for transfer. The end of the year would make a clean break."

"Sounds good," Stephen says. The dumb habit of politeness before superiors comes to him reflexively at this bad moment.

Frost hears it differently. "I'd like to kick your ass through every door from here to the lobby, smart guy."

"In effect, you already have," Stephen says, but he misses the details of Frost's explosive, curse-laden response, because thoughts of even Frost's gnarly foot . . .

*   *   *

The Borgan party is in a bland high-rise on Clark Street near the lake. Half the partygoers refer to this neighborhood as "the Gold Coast," but this is a dozen blocks north of the Gold Coast. This is the Yuppie Coast bucking for Gold Coast status. In a clingy red dress that looks like a wet sheet draped over some of the enormous rocks that line Chicago's lakefront, Doris stands at the island in the kitchen under track lighting, mixing Stephen a potent strawberry margarita.

They take their drinks out to the balcony, where the breeze is surprisingly warm for a mid-October night, just a hint of dead alewife stink wafting over from the lake. Assuming a jaunty position on the railing, Stephen accidentally swishes some margarita out of his glass, which cascades to the street below, misting the sidewalk in front of the White Hen Pantry. Likewise, he instantly spills the loss of his job at the feet of Doris.

"I deserve it," he admits. "I'm a sex addict."

"Don't clinicize yourself," Doris says. "You'll just make yourself feel bad."

"I think I'm headed for the porn industry," Stephen says glumly.

"I'm going to end up as Larry Flynt's hatchet man."

Doris hmms thoughtfully.

Stephen asks, "What about you? You don't seem bothered by what you do."

"I'm not. Everybody has something. I've got a shot glass in me right now."

"Jesus. Do you put a little pumpkin in there for Halloween?"

"Stop."

"Aren't you worried about toxic shock, or stuff like that?"

She doesn't respond. Then she murmurs: "God told me it's OK."

"He did?"

"Yeah, I prayed about it. He told me to sterilize things, if I can."

Stephen watches a thousand jokes and arguments rise and dissipate while Doris directs a steady gaze toward the downtown skyscrapers and their random patterns of light and dark windows. He decides to change the subject.

"Should we lure Richard out here and push him over the railing?"

She laughs.

"Don't you think we belong together?" he asks.

"You think it's that simple, dating a sex addict?" There's not enough irony in her voice, and his stomach clenches. "Besides, I want kids someday."

"I do have sperm, you know."

"I thought you only fuck feet."

"Yeah, but what if you held your feet close to your crotch. Like right there. I've never tried that before."

"You know, *it just might work!*" she says sarcastically, and she turns and walks inside.

* * *

Stephen has a happy and drunken holiday season, tying up loose ends at the firm. He knows he should send out his résumé right away, call the headhunters who hit on him during his successful early days at Stillwell, Hyman & Strock, but he does not do this.

01/01/01: he's unemployed. He gets out his latest 401(k) statement, takes a gander at his Fidelity Ultra Service Account. A mostly modest lifestyle (he regularly ate peanut butter sandwiches and apples for lunch at his desk), some luck playing the cycle in semiconductor stocks, other mindless tech investing (until his native sense of paranoia caused him to make massive shifts into drugs, financials, and gold throughout the first half of 2000), and he's sitting on $189,000 in his Fidelity account and $218,000 in his 401(k). No need to work right now. There's just the fetish and the getting over the fetish.

On his way to his first Sex Addicts Anonymous meeting, on a clear and cold January night in Chi-town, the sidewalks stained white with dried salt, he stops off at a porn emporium for a last wank. He finishes and there's still time to make it to the second half of the meeting, but he sees an ATM and withdraws his maximum six hundred dollars. As soon as the crisp twenties shuffle into his hands, he knows he's in for a long night. He walks down Sedgwick to North Avenue, where, despite rampant gentrification, a few prostitutes still keep the faith. He picks up the first one he sees wearing thigh-high black boots—now that it's cold, the women bring them out like winter coats. He doesn't try anything above the ankle.

Stephen would like to drink now, would like to feel fully the stringless nature of his freedom: he has money, has no place to be, has no romantic commitments. Doris is on a two-week Caribbean cruise with the Borganmeister. Stephen parks himself at a dive on Sheffield and sips toward oblivion, trying to disable his mind and body. He plans to close the place yet finds himself heading home early for a delirious three-and-a-half-hour online foot-adoration session. At 4:23 AM, he flops into bed—shattered, sweaty, smelly, sore, exhausted.

* * *

It goes on like this for months. He swings between moments when he knows he is insane and moments when he steadies his emotional wings by thinking that it hasn't been that long since he was a working member of the legal profession. His firm had been pretty high on the food chain. Not making partner there could set him up at a decent smaller firm in town, or he could become in-house counsel—maybe for Playboy Enterprises. With these legal options still plausible, he has a license to continue his binge.

Then Doris calls, out of the blue, on a warm early May day. She starts in about an article in the Sunday *New York Times Magazine* about a Prozac-style pill that can cure an out-of-control sex drive.

"Why tell me that?" Stephen asks.

"You sound weird," Doris says. "You sound like your sense of humor has been blasted right out of you."

"I need to see you. Can I see you?"

"And do what?"

"Talk about killing Richard."

"Forget it—it's over. He did something really shitty to me on that cruise." She describes how he took her out on deck one night and tried to make her hang over the railing of the ship while he masturbated.

"Let's get together and take care of each other," Stephen says.

"Yeah, right," Doris says, but they decide to go out for a drink.

* * *

It doesn't take long for them to end up at Doris's funky pad in Logan Square. Decorating motif: fighter planes. Several lampshades are emblazoned with the serrated mouths of the noses of fighter planes. There's a Snoopy and the Red Baron poster on the bathroom door; tissue and balsa-wood models, as well as plastic models, depend from wires all over the place—in dogfights, in formation, cruising alone.

Dildos are also scattered throughout the apartment like bottles in an alcoholic's house, dildos and tubes of fruit-flavored lubricants, and more strings of red and yellow beads, alternating big ones and small ones. Her apartment smells like those lubricants mixed with a loamy aroma: asshole, pussy, armpit.

"I hate my apartment," she says, as if she has nothing to do with it. She makes two screwdrivers in pint glasses, four shots of vodka per. She adds a dose of grenadine to make vodka sunrises. Nice touch. She lights expensive-smelling candles, transforming the room into a freakish den where sex between friends might happen. After the drinks, she gathers four dildos into a bouquet and asks, "Who do you want to be tonight?"

He's like a fencer choosing his rapier, or a duelist choosing his pistol—or an impotent man choosing his dildo.

"I recommend this one," Doris says. It's a strap-on model that can accommodate a limp penis inside of it. "It's perfect for you," she says without judgment, bitterness, or much apparent feeling at all.

He's not insulted yet feels the impulse to cry. He tries it, the sex, with the strap on, and it "works," in a manner of speaking. Doris lets him finish on her feet.

They lie together in bed. She asks him what's been going on, says something to the effect that his face looks plowed and left for fallow, and he tells her about the past few months—how completely out of control he is.

"It's kind of depressing," he says.

Doris explains that she isn't feeling super great, either. They commiserate. Jointly and severally, they decide the antidote is central Illinois, with its lower concentrations of prostitutes and porn emporiums, with its bleak, asexual landscape and large sky, with its purifying winds. They need to get away from all the bodies, get away from their own bodies.

They also need to wait for the weekend, because Doris is still holding down her receptionist job. But when Saturday comes, there they are, angling across the South Side on I-55, past numerous billboards for hard liquor and tropical vacations, rolling by Joliet's massive refineries, taking the bridge over the Illinois River and then straight into the heart of a million flat, greening, will-be acres of corn.

Overpasses, gentle reminders of the third dimension, arc briefly and subside. Stephen thinks of eight-year-old boys, on farms just beyond the horizon, wearing overalls and stirring mud like chocolate pudding with big sticks in long troughs. A city is like a secondary sex characteristic on the earth's body.

They stop at a Wendy's on Market Street in Bloomington, where Stephen spoons at his Frosty and Doris slurps down a plastic bowl of chili and a microwaved baked potato. She observes that Stephen is a gloomy Gus. She suggests they go all the way to St. Louis, where there are gambling boats and that big arch and a decent downtown hotel. And if they want, they'll go back to Chicago tomorrow, and if they don't want, they'll keep driving until they max out their credit cards.

Late in the afternoon, they cross the Mississippi at St. Louis, exit at Fourth Street, and follow signs for the casino boat. They go onboard the *Admiral*, an unbelievably ugly silver fortress craft: the red carpeting, the flashing and running lights, the chandeliers made of rectangular glass pieces like inverted histogram cities, the rows of shiny machines, the noise, the overall chrome-and-plush chintz all remind Stephen of a certain strip-joint chain—and he begins sweating all over his surface.

Beady-eyed Stephen sits at the craps table, rolling dice with one hand, holding a bare Doris foot, *sub tabula*, with the other. "Boxcars!" he yells. "Snake eyes!" "Threesies!" The croupier smirks and rakes in Stephen's chips. Then it's on to the slots, video poker, blackjack. They lose hundreds of dollars. They pause by the red-orange glowing buffet, gnashing greasy Buffalo wings and soggy white steak fries that they lift onto their plates with long silver tongs. When the servers come by offering drinks, they always accept. Two hours later, they wander back across the wide gangplank.

The setting sun glints off the monumental arch. They hold hands without speaking and weave their way toward it, through a narrow, nondescript park. The riverfront is unpicturesque, almost devoid of beauty, with all the atmosphere of an enormous parking lot. Between the frame of two large bridges, there are virtually no trees on the Illinois side, and the only trees on the Missouri side are in this park. You can't argue with the Arch, though—it's so big and silver and makes a pleasing shape in the air from whatever angle you see it. Huge and perfectly proportioned—just like Doris, Stephen thinks. Its two legs meet without a torso, like feet without a body.

By way of analogy with his own psyche, he sees deep into the pathology of St. Louis: an American city whose butt has been kicked, first by Chicago, then by so many other cities, a metro area that hasn't felt completely OK since the 1904 World's Fair left town, a city aware of some deep deficiency in its relationship to all other cities. It must find love and power somehow. It will make do with the Arch's gleaming, eternally spread legs.

They walk down a ramp under one of those massive legs and find themselves in a large underground room. Movie theaters abut this room, showing films about the West, about the construction of this Arch, *Monument to a Dream,* and at one end there's the entrance into a dark museum of westward expansion. The place is patrolled by park rangers in tan uniforms.

Doris and Stephen are like teenagers on their first drunk, like Shriners on holiday in Thailand, like Alice down the rabbit hole. Who would have thought there would be a whole world beneath the St. Louis Arch? Patrolled by park rangers? Ha, ha, ha, ha!

Their laughter becomes strained and out of control, filled as it is with a need for some ineffable balm to soothe their bruised souls. A well-groomed ranger approaches, but instead of bouncing them he explains that the last trips to the top of the Arch are departing soon and if they're interested, they need to get tickets right away.

Stephen gets horny. He hasn't been horny this whole trip, even though Doris is wearing sandals and cut-off jeans (she told him she inserted a tiny, glow-in-the-dark plastic Jesus to keep them chaste), but now horniness comes over him like a wave.

Their tour isn't filled, so the two of them are alone in the last car, as Stephen suspected and hoped. Their vehicle is a space-age pod with five brittle backless plastic seats, each shaped to accommodate the average ass: two sets of two opposite each other and one seat opposite the oval door. The pod is lit from behind the seats.

Doris, enormous in the small car, sits across from him. Even before the door closes, she slips off her sandals and puts her big bare feet on either side of him, a gesture almost casual, friendly, not provocative, as if she's forgotten about the fetish, as if they're longtime lovers who can fart and burp and apply medicated pads to their plantar warts together. She smiles, mimes taking a picture of him. "Click!" she says. "Perfect."

His face splits into a huge grin, as if his mouth weren't repulsively small. He becomes dimly conscious of what might possibly be the shape of something real with Doris, with whom he has felt more comfortable than with any other woman in his entire life.

Nevertheless, when the door closes, Stephen watches his hands spring his cock from his shorts. Their pod, with the turning of gears and the dropping of counterweights, ratchets up the Arch, unsmoothly, sometimes tilting with the angle of the leg, but then leveling out again. He takes Doris's feet into his hands.

"Right here, right now," he says. He gets up, forces Doris's knees back toward her chest and out, driving her feet into her crotch. His wallet and keys drag his shorts to his ankles with a thunk and a faint jingle. He needs to let go of her feet to take off her shorts, but he's too impatient and insecure; pulling aside the inseam of her cutoffs and then of her panties is barely adequate.

Doris says, "Stephen." Says it wearily, without hope of distracting him.

With pleasure receding and time running out, he persists in attempting what would be the most awkward act of intercourse in human history. He struggles to keep his penis between the soles of her feet, while also snaking this not-super-hard penis up her shorts leg and against her panties and toward a vagina containing the unsuspecting plastic Jesus. He pushes hard on her legs, trying desperately to make it work.

"You're hurting me," Doris whispers. "Stop."

The car lurches to a halt. A frisson of panic, but he must finish himself. He steps back, still holding her feet together in one sweaty hand, while working frantically with the other. The moment elongates. He sees himself: a monkey, a psychopath. But he can't stop.

Just before the operator opens their door, Doris kicks him with both feet in the chest, slamming him back into his seat. His head clunks against the polyurethane wall. The jolt reverberates through his nervous system with a sensation like guitar feedback. He becomes hell-bent on dressing himself.

The operator opens the pod door and walks on, maybe doesn't see Stephen buttoning his tented shorts. Fresh air rushes in. Doris steps into her sandals, bends and lurches, amazingly eel-like for someone her size, out the door without brushing or even grazing Stephen.

They walk up flights of stairs and into the observation room, which is dimly lit and adheres to the geometry of the Arch: the floor is narrow and humped, the carpeted walls angle up and out. Without words, they settle on opposite sides of the passage: Doris overlooks St. Louis, and Stephen overlooks St. Louis's inverse image, East St. Louis, and the rest of Illinois—the Continental Grain Company's twelve-pack of silos, the hopper and conveyor belt of

Peabody Coal. The *Casino Queen*, docked opposite the *Admiral* on the eastern shore, with its fake paddle wheel circled in yellow lights, casts its gleam on the waters of the Mississippi.

Stephen looks through the small rectangular window, his bruised head ringing. If the Arch had a face, the row of these windows would be its eyes. But it doesn't have a face. It is all leg. Or no, Stephen realizes. It's all instep. The acute arch of an enormous bound foot.

Night has fallen almost completely. He hears other tourists remark on what can be seen. He remembers feeling good and normal with Doris in the pod when she put her feet by him so casually, remembers thinking they could be together forever. He thinks he hears Doris crying—the room seems filled with the carpet-muffled sound of someone crying.

He tries to look beyond East St. Louis, across the prairie, north to big-shouldered Chicago, all the way to La Salle Street, all the way to the angels on the Board of Trade. It's time, he thinks, to really pray. There's a plastic Jesus in Doris's vagina. Off-limits now.

Moon dust is a fine, grayish, gritty soot, like combusted charcoal briquettes. Beneath the thin layer of powder, the subsoil is very hard. You don't sink into it. What a relief, because before *Apollo 11* landed, with about half a minute of fuel to spare, a few Nobel scientists had some of us at Mission Control worried that the moon's surface might not support the lunar module. We feared a sort of quicksand. But it was the long shadows and the faint grays and tans and blues the rocky landscape took on at certain distances that rooted my boots when I stood there myself, awestruck, lunar, three years later, *Apollo 16.*

Who could forget his own mother? I happen to be a man whose mother said he would forget her, after he became a big shot, a moon man.

"Mom, what can I say to reassure you? The magic words?" This was in Milwaukee, in my parents' living room, in 1972, after the parade.

"Big shots are big talkers," she'd said, her eyes darting into a raised glass of iced tea.

Now she was the one forgetting things, five months after a mild stroke, a thrombotic infarction. And the landscape out the window was big trees and grassy backyards punctuated with swing sets and pool fences, all covered in moodless midday sunshine.

We were sitting at the kitchen table, and I was telling her things about my sister, Kate, the architect; she was in Seoul, triumphant, seeing her first skyscraper go up. The soaring ambition was our coffee-fueled father's main legacy.

"As long as she's happy," Mom said, fiddling with the handkerchief that poked out of her sweater sleeve, her bony shoulders slumped, her delicate head falling forward. She had her own ideas of success. Kate was unmarried.

I nodded in vague agreement, not sure whether she was having trouble extracting the handkerchief or just worrying it. Hanging from the center of the large, rectangular window in front of us was a many-faceted glass ball that flashed blue, green, yellow, orange light from its edges.

Turned to the window, to the little glass ball, Mom left off touching the handkerchief and set down her hand, resolved. "So you came home to be with your old mush-mouth mother." She tried to say this with her dry humor, but her tongue wouldn't obey.

"Someone has to do my laundry," I said, making the expected quip.

She raised her unaffected hand to her cheek like Jack Benny and rolled her eyes. "Well, just don't make a mess of the joint."

The thickness in her voice clearly pained her, but she was fighting it. The T-shirt she wore beneath her unbuttoned sweater said: "My Son Went to the Moon and All I Got Was This Stupid Shirt." A NASA limited edition.

"Nice outfit," I said.

"It's the truth."

I laughed and waited for Mom's smile. But this time it didn't come. Instead she extended her hand toward me across the table.

The smell of too much body powder accompanied her hand and tightened my nose. My hand covered hers. I thought the moment might last overly long, so I said, "I have to get my suitcases out of the car."

"Can't stand to look at me, can you?" The sudden anger in her voice surprised me, though the doctor said she might be moody. "I can see it all over your face. Came to put me in a nursing home, didn't you?"

"I'm not going to do that."

But I had thought about it.

*   *   *

I remember Launch Day, winding our way out of the Manned Spacecraft Operations building. We wore our pressure suits and carried our portable supply units like suitcases. The oxygen flow sounded like a bicycle tire leaking in my helmet; I couldn't hear anything else. The hallways were lined with NASA people and relatives. My wife, Carol, was there. And my mother and father. Dad was smiling, but Mom looked worried, almost pained. She had something in her hands, and as I approached she flashed it at me. It was one of my baby pictures and a small wooden cross. As I walked by, she kissed both and held them to her chest. Something inside me floated loose. For a second, the hiss in my helmet sounded wrong, like a leak in the pressurized system. During the van ride to Merritt Island, I told myself, "My mother is nuts." Then it was checklist time.

*   *   *

Mom announced her afternoon nap. She preferred the couch, among all of her plants in the bright living room. During my stay,

I gathered that she was scared to death of beds. No rehab therapists were visiting, maybe because of my arrival. I thought everything would be all right if I just didn't have to help her go to the bathroom.

Divorced and childless, I'd taken a leave of absence from NASA to help her for a while, but I was toying with the idea of not going back. Nobody was sure when or if Mom would be back to normal, and there were problems in Houston—the bureaucracy, a few personalities, the shrinking budget, but mainly the fact that purpose was leaking out of what I was doing. I had worked in mission operations for the Apollo-Soyuz flight and spent most of the past seven years with the astronaut recruitment and training program. I started noticing myself bullying the recruits, telling war stories, being an asshole. I suppose some of it was boredom—maybe I'd had the same job for too long—but the real problem was I couldn't see my next move. And when my mother became sick, I got distracted. I would waste evenings, entire weekends, getting high on moon memories, fixing on scrapbooks, reading anything that might mention me. Even now, as my mom slept, I gravitated to the pictures in the hallway outside my old room.

High school graduation, delivering the valedictory. West Point class dinner, in my dress whites, receiving the Eastern Award from General Howe, honoring my combined achievement in athletics and academics. A grainier shot: on a rope bridge during Ranger school. Then I decided the classiest guys in the military were the fighter pilots. (I used to take the word "classy" seriously.) I'd had helicopter training in the Army and moved to fixed wing with the Air Force. Kennedy gave his speech, and there I was, in a graduate's robe, taking an MA in aeronautics from MIT. I met Carol in Cambridge; we grinned at me from our wedding picture. Next, the *Apollo 16* crew in black suits and skinny ties, touching a moon globe like a talisman. Then, after the span of a mere six inches of wall space, I was standing in the lunar highlands known as the Descartes region, collecting rocks with a scoop.

There were no photographs taken after 1972. To reinforce this fact, I went into my room and thoroughly unpacked every article from my suitcases into the dresser, the closet, telling myself that I might as well move back in for good. The light fell through the window in exactly the same way it had when I was a kid, and for an instant it gave me the uncanny feeling that I had never left this room, never been to the moon.

* * *

We ate dinner on the patio. Mom shifted around uncomfortably throughout the meal. She was bothered by an old back injury. Finally she threw down her napkin and said, "This body's ready for the junkyard!"

"Do you think they'd take it?"

"Oh, you're hard on me." She made a twisted, wincing smile. I took a drink of my beer, the easiest way to erase my joke. "At least I can walk," she said. "They said I wouldn't walk."

"They're always wrong."

"Do you remember?" The way she asked told me she was thinking about her back and not the stroke. Neither of us looked at the garage roof just above us. When I was eleven, she had fallen while retrieving a kite Kate had gotten stuck up there. She never forgot that.

"Sure," I said.

I remembered the pool of dark red blood around her head, how she closed her eyes hard when she spoke, comforting Kate, who was hysterical, and telling me to get a towel. First I went to the laundry room, where there was a cabinet full of towels. I had a particular type in mind; I didn't want to get her good towels all bloody. I went down the hall and into our bathroom. More of the same—plush towels, none of the old, worn-out ones I wanted. I knew time was important; I could hear Kate howling. I stepped away from the closet and tried to figure out what to do. I saw a glimpse of myself in the mirror. Seeing myself then made everything strange. I felt I had stumbled on a piece of Kryptonite. But I also felt very calm. I don't know how long I stood there; I kept thinking I should just take something and get back outside. Finally I decided to check the laundry room again. I heard a voice in the family room and detoured toward it. It was Mrs. Kraft, our neighbor, hanging up our phone. I said, "My mother fell off the roof." She said she knew that. She said not to worry, everything was going to be OK.

"What would I have done without my family then?" Mom asked.

"Well, you wouldn't have fallen in the first place."

"How'd you get to be so smart? Your mother's not so smart."

I took another drink of my beer.

"Say what?" she said.

"I didn't say anything."

"That's what I thought you said."

"Are you goofing on me, Ma?"

"Sure," she said absently.

She had been in the hospital for a few weeks with broken ver-

tebrae and a concussion. Mrs. Kraft briefed my father. He rarely
yelled at me, but I thought this time I was asking for it. I thought
he might talk about how I'd let everyone down, which was the way
he seemed to evaluate himself. He was a very intense person, had
his heart attack after a client meeting, trying to shut his stuffed
briefcase. His belly sagged against his starched white shirts like water in a balloon, but his head was impressive. His profile reminded
me of a football lineman wearing his helmet, though his face was
fleshy and manly in an indoor way. It was a great head for a corporate lawyer, and I loved to look at it. I imagined that head brooding
over what I'd done, worrying about whether I would amount to anything, searching for the words to talk some sense into me. I wanted
to ask him about the Kryptonite feeling. But he never spoke to me
about the accident.

So Mom and I sat there on the patio, in June, thirty-five years
after the fall, and I wanted to change the subject.

The sun was nearly down, and her yard was filling with shadows. The lawn and the evergreen shrubs were badly overgrown,
like a perfectly handsome face that had gone hairy, distorted, were-
wolf. The only clouds were high milky sheets that blended with the
light blue of the sky. The moon, in its last quarter, had risen. Barely
visible on its inner curve was the Ocean of Storms, landing site of
Apollo 12. I turned to tell Mom this, but she'd fallen asleep.

Night was coming—or, we were rotating into a darkness. On the
moon, darkness is a place; you have to seek it out. On the Earth, it's
a time; you can't get away from it.

Later, I tucked her in bed. She asked me to leave the door open
and the hall light on.

* * *

After we land on the moon, there's a scheduled rest period before
our first EVA (extra-vehicular activity). John Young and I get permis-
sion to remove our moon cocoons and go to bed in the buff. (Pressure suits are hell to sleep in if there's any kind of gravity involved.)
Before going to sleep, I pull two photographs out of my personal
preference kit. They're in the same plastic holder, back to back: one
of my parents, one of my wife. Moonstruck, I get sentimental; I will
leave the pictures on the lunar surface. I want to leave my parents'
picture because part of the reason I've come to the moon is to take
them here. I want to leave Carol's picture because things are awful between us and I need to leave her behind. With this resolved,
I sleep surprisingly well. I wake up on the moon naked and well
rested. I feel like a newborn.

* * *

The next morning I fixed Mom a breakfast of cantaloupe and Cheerios. Afterward, an hour with the paper, minutes with junk mail, getting water, finding Mom's shoes, the TV, another meal.

   In the early afternoon, I picked up the booklet the physical therapist had left, put down the mat in the living room, and told my
mother it was time for her exercises.

   She killed the TV with the remote and struggled to sit up. "It's
exercise getting off the sofa," she said.

   "OK, Ma, lie down on your stomach."

   "Oh, this is rich! 'Lie down, Ma,' my foot. You're going to tie me
up and take me to that nursing home." She inched her hips off the
cushion, holding to the arm of the couch with both hands like a

swimmer easing into a pool. Just before her knees reached the carpet, she slipped from her seat and fell with a thud. I took a sharp breath, but she simply crawled onto the mat and lay down. "Now what?" she asked, with what I took to be mock belligerence.

"Put your weight on your elbows and forearms."

"Oh, for crying out loud!"

"OK," I said, reading from the exercise book. "Now extend your right arm in front of you."

There was a pause while she decided which one was her right. Then she extended it, bearing her weight on her affected elbow and forearm. Her back brace made a ridge under her sweatshirt.

"Very good," I said. "You're really doing good."

We progressed through kneeling, sitting, and standing exercises. She remembered how to do some of them on her own.

When we finished, she whispered, "Thank you." Then she sank down on the couch and started to cry. "I want my body back," she managed.

I sat next to her. I put my hand on her back but touched only the brace. "You'll get better," I said, and I rubbed the brace.

*   *   *

I drive the rover toward Smokey Mountain, through boulder fields, across cratered, undulating terrain. Feeling excited, I am proceeding a little recklessly, even though the jouncing has already broken the instrument on the rover that indicates the vehicle's degree of roll. We approach a boulder as big as my parents' house, probably ejected from the impact that formed a nearby six-hundred-foot-deep crater. It's the largest rock we've seen on the moon. John whistles. The thrill is indescribable. This moment is the mission, I think. I stop the rover and we go over and touch the huge rock. I leave the pictures there.

*   *   *

For a few weeks, we settled into a routine. I handled her physical therapy and her occupational therapy, and a speech therapist came by once a week. In the evenings, there was rummy or TV. While she napped, I tried to read Churchill's history of the Second World War, but I inevitably thought about my "next move." Mom had always said, "They've already been to the moon. The only place you need to go is back to church." (She was a serious Catholic herself, always visiting the sick, baking for retarded kids, stuffing envelopes. But I knew her motherly ego had gotten the best of her at least once: Kate told me Mom was crying for joy, proud as Satan, when I walked on the moon.) Sometimes I was excited about leaving the agency, about the possibility of "doing something good," as Mom would say, and other times both leaving and staying seemed pointless. It was like the old Kryptonite feeling.

*   *   *

In one scrapbook there was the shot of Nixon and me in the East Room. His handshake was extremely firm, the arm not fully extended, so I had to stand closer to him than I wanted. He asked if I'd be willing to campaign for him in the Wisconsin primary. I laughed and said I'd feel like a complete idiot giving a political speech. As he took this in, he moved his left eye down toward me (he was several inches taller than I was, to my surprise), as if it had special powers of persuasion or were his only eye that worked. Then I felt his hand on my back and he was asking me, "Have you had a chance to talk with

P. N.?" (His wife, it turned out.) Carol was furious with me for turning down the president. We had an awful fight. Still, we traveled together to Milwaukee for a hometown parade, rode down Wisconsin Avenue, smiling and waving. Despite perfect weather, the turnout was lousy. By *Apollo 16*, moon landings were no longer such big news. The largest bulge of spectators was on the steps of the public library, but later I found out this was several grade-school field trips stranded because their buses couldn't cross the parade route. The mission was definitely over. Within a year, so was the marriage.

* * *

One evening, the local Cubmaster, Fred Walsh, phoned. He had heard I was back in town, asked if I'd be willing to judge this year's Cub Scout pinewood derby, said it would really be something. The kids had carved rubber band–powered model rocket ships. At the church festival in 1972, I posed for pictures for a dollar a crack and swore I would never do anything like that again. But I told Fred I'd be glad to.

Mom had been in a slump, and on the night of the pinewood derby she wanted me to put her in bed before I left.

I pulled the covers up to her chin, smiling blandly. Her weakness and disorientation of the past few days scared me. I was eager to get out of that room, but her unaffected hand slipped out and pulled the blanket away from her neck, like a person putting a foot in a closing door. "Matthew," she said. "What was your father like? You know I try, I have the pictures."

Lately her brain seemed to be draining through a sieve.

"He was good," I said, without thinking. "He worked very hard. He had his problems. He was more sensitive than people think. You should be proud of him."

"But what was he like? What kinds of things did he say?"

The creeping desperation in her voice made me wish I had a joke handy, but I didn't. "He wasn't as funny as you, but he laughed at your jokes. He said he loved you."

"In front of you kids?" Her eyes went wide with disbelief.

"Sure," I said, lying.

"I doubt it," she said, and closed her eyes. "Give your mother a kiss."

* * *

Cub Pack 552 convened in the Sacred Heart church hall. All the young Tiger Cubs, Wolves, Bears, and Webelos were in full dress blues, replete with pack insignia, activity badges indicating Naturalist, Scholar, Aquanaut. During the Pack meeting, Walsh introduced me as an Air Force colonel and former astronaut. The kids' eyes lit up. I could see them making the connection between the rockets they'd built and my credentials. But my mind drifted back to my mother. At that moment, she was probably crawling out of bed to look for pictures of her husband. I shouldn't have left her. I felt ridiculous before the Scouts, angling for the approval of these tiny, prepubescent men. Walsh asked me to say a few words.

I rose slowly. I should have expected this, but just then there was no reasonable speech in my head. The Scouts sat straight-backed, some literally on the edge of their folding chairs. I said this: "I was a Scout, just like you!" Silence resumed. I scanned the small, soft, shiny faces. What to say? A quote from Churchill? Vince Lombardi? The truest things I knew were that I was overwhelmed by memories of time spent on the lunar surface, that I was addicted to memorabilia, that my mother frightened me, that in odd moments I confused her with the moon. The round faces shimmered, wavered, like coins in a pool. The moment was stuck and I waited for something to unstick it. "Play fair," I told them, and I sat down.

Walsh, a toastmaster's toastmaster, thanked me and glibly moved to the next item on the program. Many Scouts continued to stare at me, some with curiosity and others with the sour mouths of the cheated. I had to restrain a strange yip or yelp rising in my throat, a bubble of emotion escaping like a burp. It was almost comical—yet alarming, too. But I got a grip. I sat tight.

Near the end, Carol said she knew something was wrong with us when she realized she couldn't have a child with me. There was something closed about me, she said, something that really hit her watching me on TV. Seeing me in the pressure suit with the helmet over my head scared her because it felt familiar; it was how she had always known me. The fact was, she made me nervous. She had been a model, had made pots of money in real estate. She was smart and beautiful, and I wore her pinned to my side like a medal, but she made me nervous. Our personalities didn't go together, which I had never imagined could be a problem. And, if the truth be known, I was no mission specialist in the sack.

Now I wondered what it would be like to teach high school history, coach the track team—pursuits, I was embarrassed to admit, I used to consider beneath me. I wanted to do something undriven by ambition, jealousy, or selfishness. By the time I returned home, I was excited enough to tell my mother. Maybe she would wake up in the middle of the night, since she went to bed so early.

I took a seat in the living room, where, if I twisted my neck, I could see down the hall into my mother's room at a sign of her rous-

ing, and I read from my Churchill. I drifted into scenes of present-
ing the Italian campaign in a classroom.

Then I heard my mother moving on her bed. I stood, hoping she
might be waking up, but the movement sounded strange. I took a
few steps, paused, listened, and then walked quickly to her room,
flicked on the light. Her legs, her arms, her whole body was vibrating violently, her half-closed eyes were rolled back in her head, and
the right side of her upper lip was curled in a sneer.

"She's having a seizure," I said, as if speaking to Mission Control.
I hovered for an instant but then rushed to the phone on the nightstand, called an ambulance. When I hung up, she was still shaking.
The person on the phone hadn't given me any instructions except
to wait there.

"You're OK, Ma, you're OK." I wanted to touch her, to make it
stop, but I was afraid. "You're OK, Ma."

An agonized gurgle escaped her mouth, then I smelled urine and
feces. I thought that when she stopped moving, I would clean her, I
would carry her in my arms to her seat in the shower, I would care
for her.

But the trembling wouldn't stop. I inched toward her, leaned
over, and extended my hands slowly as if fearful of an electric shock.
Before I could touch her shoulders, she became still. I exhaled and
stood over her for several minutes, watching her stricken face. Then
I heard the siren and ran into the living room.

*   *   *

In the final hours of our moon visit, we return to our squat module
and I remember the 363-foot rocket, the 7.5 million pounds of thrust
that sent us here. I think: someone has miscalculated. It seems there

is no way the tiny module can send us on our way home. But no matter what the mistake, somehow I will make up the difference, I will get us home. This is known as rising to the occasion. Failure in space can be pinpointed: there is an instant when things become irrevocably wrong. If I had made a two-second mistake in our final engine burn over the lunar surface, we would have missed the moon entirely. Death would not have happened right away, but it would have been guaranteed. By now our bodies would be on their way past Neptune.

*   *   *

In the waiting room, I watched a late-night movie starring Jackie Cooper, one of my mother's favorites. After about an hour, the doctor came out. He was young and handsome, a light-skinned black man who spoke in a terse, confident voice. To match this, I assumed a faintly military posture, clipped my speech a bit, but abandoned this as he went on. He said Mom's condition had stabilized. He said a seizure like this can happen when scar tissue forms on the damaged part of the brain. The seizure was mild, commensurate with her stroke. Still, it was a demoralizing setback and she was going to be in the hospital for a while. She was resting now and I should, too, so I would be fresh when I came to visit her tomorrow. Then he told me not to worry.

I got home around 3:00 AM, stripped her bed, put everything into the wash. I scrubbed her mattress. Then I meandered about the house until I found myself in the dark kitchen, looking out the window. Her glass ball hung there, where it's been for more than twenty years, right about at the level of her eyes, her lips. The moon was obscured by clouds, but I knew it was floating somewhere in front of me. I wondered if this glass ball meant anything to her or if what it once meant had been forgotten. I wondered if I would ever tell her that her picture is on the moon, back to back with that of another woman I tried to leave behind there. Imagining the moon, thinking of her, I bent over and kissed the ball, so lightly it barely moved. Then I stepped back. In the shadow, her globe hovered in the air, seemingly without support, suspended apart from all other things by unseen forces. It never rested; it just hung there, waiting for someone to arrive, to touch down.

He went to the Li'l Peach to get some milk and see her again. It had been an entire week since he'd last been there and seen her and done it with her. He let a man who came up to the counter at the same time go ahead of him. She smiled at him faintly, over the man's hairy head. He could almost convince himself that her straight gray hair, parted in the center and swinging like beads when she moved, was really platinum blonde. When another customer came in, she made a little frown. He stepped away from the counter, stalling until the new customer got his cigarettes and left. But then the wife of one of the owners came in, a little early tonight. He finally went to the counter with his milk.

"Hi there," she said.

"Hey," he said, and they both laughed a little.

"Nothing like good old milk," she added, deadpan.

He laughed nervously, his mind all tied up with what to say.

When she handed him his change, her bunched fingers touched his palm. He stopped thinking about how old she was.

She reached under the counter and pulled out a fat white envelope. "Here you go," she said.

On the front of the envelope was the word "You."

He felt the pressure of another customer behind him. "OK," he said. "Thanks a lot." He met her eyes, and she looked back at him in a way that was both empty and full, as if she were staring into space but right at him. "See you."

On his way home, feeling the envelope's thickness, he imagined it contained a long and crazy profession of love. Or maybe she had just written a very short message in huge words. Above all he wanted to know what she thought of him and how he looked to her.

He waited until he had put away the milk and said good night to his mom and secured himself in his room before he opened the letter. Her first words reassured him: "Dear Lover."

He read on:

"The first thing I want you to know is that I have no cats or dogs. I think this is important to tell you. I also want you to know that I am not as old as I look. I am forty-one, only about three times as old as you.

"I don't think you realize what we've done. I feel I have to tell you everything, so that you'll see.

"I'm afraid I need to tell you that I grew up on a landing at the top of the stairs of a triple-decker on Washington, right outside the apartment where my mother and father and two sisters lived. I slept in a storage closet with an accordion door that closed on a magnetic latch.

"I ended up there because my parents fought a lot. Most of the fights my mom just yelled. Yelled and yelled. My dad never yelled back. If she brought up the mice in the stove, or the light on the porch, or the hole in the screen door, he'd say he'd get to it and she would say he always said that. And he *would* get to it—except when he wanted to spite her. But she picked fights not really because he did anything wrong but because she wanted him to get close to her.

So one time she was yelling at him in their bedroom and all of a sudden he yelled back: 'It's because you're so fat. How do you expect me to get it up when you look like that?'

"He actually said that to her. Me and my two sisters, we heard it in our room. My two older sisters thought it was funny—Mom and Dad fighting about sex. I didn't laugh though. I started crying.

"They called me a crybaby but I couldn't stop. I told them to shut up, they told me to cut off my head and grow a scab. We had our own fight until Dad pounded on our door and said to go to sleep.

"We did. When I woke up in the middle of the night, I had to pee, so I went out into the living room and saw Dad asleep on the couch. He was on his back with his arms folded over his chest like a mummy. I went to the bathroom and he was there on the couch when I went back to the bedroom. I didn't know why but I wet the bed that night. I was so surprised, I told my sisters. This time they didn't laugh. They got real serious and told Mom."

He lowered the letter and looked around his room. The apartment was very quiet. His mom had turned off the TV and gone to bed. She said good night through the door now. She used to walk right in.

"She was a wreck—no sleep," the letter went on. "Yelled and yelled. And the next night the same thing happened. This time Mom and Dad both yelled. Mom said I was ruining the bed. My sisters said I smelled bad and had a disease.

"They tried a lot of things that didn't work: sleeping with my feet higher than the rest of me, not drinking fluids after 7:00 PM, setting an alarm so I could pee in the middle of the night (which of course my sisters complained about, too), but nothing worked. Finally Mom cleaned out the closet on the landing. She put some flattened boxes down on the floor, to protect the scuzzy wooden planks from my pee, and gave me an old air mattress to lie on. So I slept in the closet one night.

"Sure enough, I didn't wet the bed sleeping on the landing, and we all thought I was cured. I was so relieved, I was glad to be on the landing instead of in our apartment. I didn't think twice about it. They let me in for meals, and sometimes TV, and of course to do my chores, but I gradually moved my favorite stuff out to the landing and had a little clubhouse. There was even a window where I could stare out for hours without my sisters mocking me. I watched the streetlights flicker on at night and I spied on the people across the street as they watched TV. It was OK."

He read with growing disappointment. The letter wasn't about him at all. Though she couldn't have known he'd been a virgin, he expected her at least to mention what they'd done, how he had showed her that he was as much a man as any man could be. But it seemed that the whole letter would be about her miserable child-hood.

"And the thing was," he read on, "Mom and Dad didn't feel guilty. In fact, Mom was real proud of herself for thinking up the miracu-lous closet treatment. She lost a little weight. She and Dad didn't fight so much—they just weren't as pissed off. After fifteen years of marriage, they found out they both liked to play Crazy Eights.

"Then they started screwing on the front porch, right in front of my eyes and everyone else's. We lived right on the bus line. There was traffic going by practically every second. First the Crazy Eights, then she sat on his lap and wiggled like the seat was uncomfortable. In the beginning, I didn't know they were doing it, but the second year I was on the landing—I was eleven by then—I figured out what was going on. She didn't wear skirts, maybe because they liked to do it front to back and even just hitching up her skirt would maybe be too revealing. Instead, she made alterations to her pants—a flap where needed. They did it year round, even in the winter when there was snow on the porch and they had to clean off the chair they shared with a broom."

He read that part again. "Oh my God," he whispered. He was starting to understand. Her pants had been that way.

"Things got great around the house. My sisters stopped abusing me; they acted like they owed me something. My folks almost never had fights. On Sundays we'd make a big bowl of popcorn and watch *The Wonderful World of Disney.* We hung out at the dinner table, talking and laughing. I found out my Dad used to play piano for a vaudeville act. From the way he remembered those bits, he could have been one of the actors. Mom had shown champion dogs at one time—basset hounds—for a rich old aunt. Do you know that basset hounds have been bred to be so long and low to the ground that they can't even mate normally anymore? Imagine that. People have to lift the male and then hold both dogs together til it's done. Anyway, my parents bought a used upright piano. Good feelings were coming out of the woodwork faster than the roaches.

"I even found out why I really wet the bed. It was the old dunk-the-hand-in-a-bowl-of-water trick" (*She's lying,* he thought) "and it worked on me because I'm such a heavy sleeper. Roberta—she's my almost nice sister—she told me when everything was good.

"At first I was mad. I wanted to tell Mom and Dad and get back in the house. It was embarrassing when my friends came over and saw my storage closet. But my sisters said they would deny my story, and if I did get back in their room they would pull the trick on me again. That room was always too cramped for the three of us, and it would be even worse now that we were teenagers. The problem was Dad's meter reader salary, and his trips to the Wonderland track, which is what made us live in such a small place and helped cause all of those splendid fights. But now it was like we had a three-bedroom apartment. We were all feeling more respectable.

"My sisters kept putting me off. They told me to at least wait another month before trying to ruin everything. But after a while they knew that even I didn't want to get my way. Then over—I swear—interlocked fingers at the breakfast table, Dad told us that Mom had two, maybe three, eggs left before she passed over into infertility, and they were trying to make a baby brother for us. Nothing against you girls, he said, but he'd always wanted a son. 'Where will he sleep?' Tammy, my more evil sister, asked. 'Doesn't matter,' Mom and Dad said practically in unison. I watched for a change in their porch maneuvers and found it: afterward, Mom lay on her back and raised her hips on a set of pillows. I caught the two of them eyeing the sparrows' nest in the busted-out porch light. The mother bird bringing worms for her young inspired our parents to further attempts at fertilization.

"So it went on as good as anyone could possibly imagine. Until new people, nosy people, moved in on the second floor. When their calico cat, Maurice, stepped into my closet to sleep with me, they found out I was living on the landing. Next thing we knew the landlord decided to pay a friendly call.

"He sat on our long gold couch, wearing a trench coat that he never took off and twirling a Humphrey Bogart hat in his hands. Dad sat in his chair opposite and I hunched in the other chair, a little apart, and my mom and my two sisters stood there watching.

Everybody sort of looked at the coffee table while our landlord talked. He had a beautiful voice and a soft tan face. His hair was gray but he was very handsome. His shoes were shiny and the crease of his pants was sharp enough to slice cheese.

"Despite what we all said, the landlord thought he'd found a very sad situation. And I did look sort of grubby in my sisters' hand-me-downs, and my hair did start streaking with gray when I was only twelve, and I did sometimes let my used sanitary napkins accumulate in a plastic bag in the closet instead of throwing them away or changing them during the day in a bathroom like a regular person. But still. I told him I liked living on the landing very much.

"Then he said he wanted to have a private talk with our parents. And me and my sisters went into the bedroom where we could hear everything anyway. The landlord said he believed in our neighborhood and that he believed in us. He said he had believed in our neighborhood when other people had stopped believing. He said that in a neighborhood of good feelings everyone looked out for one another and lived as best as they could. Our parents said that they also believed in these things. He said that 'in large part' the way we lived was none of his business but it seemed to him that it just wasn't right or natural for a child to live in his storage closet. Looking at it financially—and he wasn't out for our last dime, like some landlords—the city inspector could possibly fine him thousands of dollars. And then Dad said that our landlord could send in the National Guard and a whole army of city inspectors, but he would reserve the right to see his family live as he saw fit in the space he paid good money every month to rent. And then the landlord said that now that he mentioned it, my dad should know that our rent was kept artificially low by our landlord's wish to help a family that seemed to need it, but if a family was resistant to help and instead wanted to cause problems, then he might have to raise the rent to its fair market level and let the chips fall where they may. Certainly, though, tearing down the closet would allow the rent to remain the same. Or maybe our parents might voluntarily take steps? Then the landlord said this was all he had come to talk about and he hoped everyone would enjoy the remainder of the weekend.

"For days my father brooded about the landlord's visit, blaming him for all the problems a meter reader's family might get into, even when the meter reader also travels to Wonderland on a regular basis. But it seemed to me that I could smell the smell of the landlord's aftershave very easily after that. I had a fantasy in which he came by one day and asked me to live with him and make him dinner. Then after I did a good job of making dinner, he would take me out to dinner, and after I'd done a good job of eating dinner, he would take me to a movie, and if I sat quietly enough he would put his arm around me and kiss the top of my head and say that I was his now and it was time for me to make demands on his generosity. Now that he knew I was living on the landing, it seemed to me that a visit from him, one my parents would not know about, was very likely.

"That's when I started hearing stuff, at night. The door would open downstairs. I would listen for keys in a lock, the first-floor people, the second-floor people. I knew the sound of their keys, how they took the stairs. But for a few nights I heard the door open, and then nothing. Nobody ever came up the stairs to those other apartments. I wondered if I heard right. One night I was going crazy, waiting for the person who opened the door to do something, so I went all the way down the stairs, shaking like a leaf in my nightie.

Nobody there. But the door was open a little.

"Then there was the night when I heard the door open, and I thought it was just the wind. I was going to go down and shut it right away, instead of lying there listening for imaginary sounds. I stood up but caught my breath because it seemed as if I heard very quiet steps on the stairs. Steps so quiet you think maybe you're making them up, but there *is* a sound in your head, the sound of somebody trying to make no sound, on steps. I gripped my nightie in my hands. My heart became loud. The man—I knew it was a man of some kind—the man coming up the stairs knew those stairs so well that he could step without making a creak. Who could know our stairs so well? I tried to hold myself totally still so I could listen even harder, sending my ears up and down the steps to pick up where the sound was now. And when it was so quiet that I knew I could never move again, that's when I heard the scrape of a heavy shoe on the landing right outside my little room. And then, I swear to God, I heard something breathing fast, almost panting like a dog. The breathing clogged my ears and before I knew it I was screaming and could not stop. I jerked up the window and ripped out the screen and rolled over the sill and onto the porch. I yanked open the porch door, then pulled the inside door but I should have been pushing, screaming the whole time. Finally I got in and ran toward the bathroom, but then my mom was there and I was in her arms.

"It was fifteen minutes before I could tell anyone what happened. Dad went down to check on the door and said it was wide open, the landlord was going to hear about *this*. I was pretty hysterical, pulling on my own hair and crying. My sisters stood around until they got tired of watching and I still cried, and finally Mom pushed me into my sisters' room and told me to sleep in my old bed. The next morning we all vowed that we'd do our best with me living in the apartment again.

"And for a while we did all right. But three teenage girls in one room, and Tammy telling Mom how she *didn't* cure me and Mom putting on weight again, everything just . . . The little brother never came, even though I wanted him to. I thought I could be his special nurse and protector. I would volunteer to change and feed him, to live with him out in the closet. But my parents lost their special baby-making powers. The fact is, everything's delicate. There are only a few situations in life when things get happy. For a while our family had such a situation, but then certain circumstances came along.

"Why am I telling you all this? Maybe I don't exactly know—"

"Come on," he said out loud, speaking to the page. "What is this shit?" The more he heard about her, the more he needed her to say something about him. His impatience had an edge of panic. He felt like a kite rising in a strong wind.

"But maybe I do know what you're up against now," she went on, "thinking about the love we've had so far, wondering how much more love can be had and at what risk. The problem with my family's happy situation was that some people didn't like it. They probably thought it wasn't 'normal.' But let me tell you, lover, you should beware of trying to be happy with the way things are normally done.

"All my life, it now seems to me, from the closet onward, has been a search off the beaten path. I have been in some college classes. I have glued plastic daisies onto green welcome mats of plastic grass. I have lived in Paris, France, in the 19th, on the Avenue Mathuria Moreau with a man who turned out to be kind and generous but very bad, too. I remember the last rainy sick February morning I stayed with him. He was a great fan of the American West and taught me how to shoot. He said he didn't belong in Paris but that's where he lived, working for a bank, trading currencies. I can still see him in his bikini briefs, shivering on the radiator before the open window, going back and forth between screaming and laughing, the air outside a cold mist that went right into you. I never did get married, though I could have. I studied Buddhism for a while in Charleston, South Carolina, with a Tibetan monk. I have even studied the Tibetan language and know many of its phrasings. But I came back to Somerville when my parents died. My sisters were long gone. I got a job at the Li'l Peach, right near the high school where you must go, though I don't know that for sure.

"I want you to know how special you are."

"Finally," he said. He laughed with relief, then laughed at himself for how relieved he was. He could forgive her the whole stupid letter for writing that.

"We all have fantasies," she continued, "and when one of them comes true, we need to stop and think about what it means. I have been working at the Li'l Peach for three years. One night last spring when I was working with Rafi and he was putting milk in the cooler in the back, I got the idea of making the adjustments to my pants that you are now familiar with. There is a period on weeknights, between 10:45 and 11:15, when the store gets very quiet, before things pick up again before closing. I don't know why this is, but it is. During this time, Rafi stocks the shelves and the coolers, and then at 11:15 one of his brothers, and sometimes one or two of the wives, shows up to help guard the register and take the money. Maybe you've seen this? What happened to me was that when I stood by

myself in the quiet store I began to think of my childhood days in
the closet (which is just a five-minute walk from where I am writing this now, a ten-minute walk from the Li'l Peach), and I began to
have fantasies of a man coming in the empty store when Rafi was in
back and of this man wanting to have sexual intercourse with me
very quickly. I did not really think this would ever happen. It was a
fantasy, but I prepared myself for it by altering my pants, by buying
crotchless panties from a famous Hollywood outlet. It seemed the
most unlikely fantasy to ever come true.

"I remember when I thought it could come true with you. I had
seen you in the store during the day with your friends. You told a
lot of jokes with them, and you looked happy. That's when I first
noticed you. But I really knew you were special when you came in
by yourself one night. When nobody is buying anything, I stand
very still behind the counter with my hands floating away from my
sides like I'm a gunslinger. Rafi doesn't like this—he says it makes
the customers nervous, and it usually does, but not you. Something
in your expression when you came to the counter said you understood. Plus I knew there was a family behind your errands and I
imagined it was like the family I grew up in. I could tell by the condition of the money you handed me: the crumpled bills for Nyquil,
a handful of coins to buy milk. You probably think it had to do with
your body, but it's just that I thought I could make you see. Does
this make any sense?

"And then tonight you came in and went up and down the aisles,
like you didn't know what you wanted. You stopped in front of me
and wouldn't look at me, but studied the rows of candy. I saw you
glance at the porn magazines in their dark plastic pouches at the
side of the counter, and I smiled to let you know this was OK, but

you didn't react. I hoped you would try to buy one, because then everything would have been obvious. But you went away from the counter, like you needed a running start to leap to me. You went to the soda fountain and got a small soda and brought it to me, to pay for it with your warm and sweaty coins. I let my hands float onto the counter, palms down, ignoring for a second your outstretched hand full of coins. This is how you knew. I let my hands sit on the counter, with the safe side up, and I smiled at you, and tilted my head a little, and let my . . . I knew you were my lover when you reached out your left hand and touched the top of my right hand. And I moved into your touch like a cat would. Then I turned my hands over, exposing the soft and dangerous interior of my palms to you. We clasped our hands together, even your hand with the coins in it, and I lifted our hands into the air, as a few coins dropped and rolled, and danced us down to the end of the counter, and lifted our hands over the sunglasses display, and pulled you over to my side. We stayed near the end, so you could slip away, down the single step and out the door if Rafi finished putting milk in the cooler. I bent over and undid my snaps and you knew what to do, bless your heart.

"But now, after levitating for a long moment above the aisles and counters of the Li'l Peach, we have landed and there is time for a few questions. Now that you know some important things about me, what do you say? You know that I can take chances, that I am a good lay, that though I look old I am not quite that old, that I can make your young blood boil. This should be enough for a start, don't you think? I feel we can both change our lives, if we're willing to be bold. I wish you could see this.

"So what do you say? Do you like me? Do you think we could

ever be in love? I live at 72 Dane Street, right across from the Maaco garage, in a small apartment at the top of the stairs. The night after you get this I'll leave the doors open. Please come over. Don't ring the bell, just walk right in. I'll be waiting for you.

Maureen"

He folded the letter and lay back on his bed. He tried to simply hang on to the fact of the letter, but something about what she had written was rushing him forward. She had written so much. None of it matched what he had thought about her after they had done it. In his diary, he had written, "It's the greatest thing that has ever happened to me. All that time getting nowhere with girls at school and now all of a sudden this happens. I have entered manhood." Then he'd added, "Maybe I've just used and abused her, but she didn't seem to mind. She wanted it! Horny old bitch. I can't believe it."

Even as he wrote "bitch," he had regretted it—he didn't mean it. But he felt sort of rough and tough thinking about what he had done, and it was only his diary. He had waited a whole week before going to see her again, as a kind of penance (even though he didn't believe in all that junk anymore), and to savor the first time.

He read the letter again. There was something scary and depressing about it. When he got to the part where she described how they had done it, he thought of masturbating, but he didn't. Her words made him uneasy. He started to write a letter to her on a page in one of his school notebooks. "Dear Lover," he wrote. "I am fifteen years old. I am as old as I look. Ha, ha." But he crossed out "Ha, ha." It was immature. Then he crossed out "I am as old as I look." He didn't

know how to joke with her. He read the first few pages of the letter
again. Then he went on: "I have lived in Somerville all my life. I am
an only child. I live with my mother. She is an x-ray technician at
Mass General. My father lives in Philadelphia." He stopped writing
and read through the rest of her letter. Then he lay back with his
hands behind his head, staring around his room.

The only poster on his walls was of a pair of skiers, photographed
from the air, racing down a snowy mountainside. He was not interested in skiing but had found the poster in his closet when they
moved in. He didn't have any other posters up. All of his friends
put up posters of the things and people they liked, until the walls
of their rooms were a collage of posters. He could never seem to
like something that much. Once he had gotten a small poster of a
band inside a CD, and he put that up, but it embarrassed him after a
while and he took it down. Now he stared at the poster of the skiers
and wondered who had bought it, what they had liked about it, and
why they had left it behind. If he ever had a poster he liked enough
to put up, he would never just forget about it.

He read the letter again.

He wondered why the letter made him feel lonely and a little
scared. Her life fascinated him but it was so sad. "Your life fascinates
me, but it is so sad," he added to his letter to her. But he couldn't
write that. His letter was completely ruined. And it wasn't just the
letter that was ruined; this feeling about her, which he could never
tell her, was between them now. To think of her waiting for him
behind the counter of the Li'l Peach was one thing, to think about
being with her in her life was something else. It all made him want
to escape from her and be with his friends. But it was too late to call
someone.

At 1:00 AM, he went to bed, even though he wasn't tired. In the darkness, he rolled over to where she might be someday. She had charged up everything about his life, and he couldn't let go of her. If only she weren't so old, he thought. She was too old, older than his mother, who stayed away from him now, as if he were a bomb. Was that what scared him? Forty-one wasn't *that* old, if she weren't lying about it. He wished he had met her when she was living in the closet and it was he who snuck up the stairs every night to be with her, and they had fallen in love and he had somehow stopped her from becoming an old woman with a hole in her pants who worked at the Li'l Peach.

With the lights out, he couldn't read the letter again, but he found it there in his mind, her voice reading it to him, saying it. He heard her talk about life in the closet, about a strange man in Paris, about her fantasy, and her hopes for him. She seemed to be challenging him in some way, and that bothered him.

For the first time in his life, he wasn't able to fall asleep. He turned over and over, overheating his pillow, getting mad because tonight he really cared about getting to sleep so he could forget her for a while. But there was no escaping. Should he go to her again? Was there something wrong with him for fucking an old lady in public? Did that mean his life would be as sad and as strange as hers? A vague sense of resentment filtered through him, a feeling of violation, almost, which he couldn't account for but which got stronger as he kept thinking. Why did she write so much? This really made him mad—how much she had written. About her pee and her sanitary napkins. Did he have to know this? A man shivering, a dog breathing. He turned himself over again. And again.

When the sun came through his window, he woke up. All night

he had been conscious of being in his bed, with thoughts of Maureen running through his mind, but now he was fully aware of the room and knew that what had come before must have been sleep, though this sleep had brought no rest or even the sense that his train of thought had been broken. It was much worse than waking up on the morning of a test. The letter lay open on his nightstand, the thick trifold making the paper stand up on both ends. He was instantly drawn back to it, leaned over, and saw the first line: "Dear Lover."

These words, which had made him happy the first time he read them, now made him sit up quickly. He tore the letter into small pieces. Then he lay back on his bed and tried to breathe easily. The sharp sound of tearing paper died away slowly. As silence settled on his room again, he could still feel her words moving inside him, like soldiers dropped from the belly of a Trojan horse. Then, even though he wanted very much to get away from her, he knew how she had felt when she stood in her closet and the sound had come to the top of the stairs and had scraped and become the panting of a dog. He knew exactly how she had felt. It was a terrible feeling. When they had stood coupled behind the counter of the Li'l Peach, he didn't know he was touching this feeling. It didn't feel at all like manhood was supposed to feel, this feeling.

The Women Were Leaving the Men

The men weren't obviously bad—not in any way visible from the outside—but the women were leaving them. The women who left the men had money, were lawyers, were doctors, were tenured professors; the women who left the men were not so well off, worked at JCPenney, answered the phones for plumbing contractors, toiled as adjunct instructors, actually had unsteady financial prospects but were leaving anyway. They were not leaving the men as women had left men in the previous generation, with a sense of breaking out of prison, or smashing something evil and oppressive, or opening their eyes after years of blindness, or because they were finally deciding for themselves. Yes, there were still some women who left their philandering gynecologist husbands in the traditional way: outraged, victimized. But something new had been happening, and the men didn't understand what it was.

The women said things like, "I just don't want to be married to you anymore." They said, "I need a new space. I need a home that feels like I made it."

The women left men who were doing their half—or nearly their half—of the child care, who had uncomfortable relationships with their own fathers on which they brooded, who tried to correct these matters by being good fathers themselves. These men caulked windows, built 401(k)s, and opened cans in the kitchen; they congratulated their toddlers upon delivering bowel movements into the potty. Many of these men held white-collar jobs that did not appear in children's books when they were growing up: database administrator, client services representative, partner in a company that installs telecommunication products and services. Great fathers, by many measures. The husbands their mothers had always really wanted.

The women left men with whom they had gone through many levels of higher education, men who had taken the presence of women in colleges, in med schools or law schools, or even in chemistry PhD programs as a given. These men had older relatives who made them squirm with their unreconstructed maleness—with their "what's the difference between a woman and a Kleenex" jokes and their tales of salesmen talked down and engines rebuilt, all spoken into beer cans held like microphones. The men had denounced these relatives to their spouses, had apologized for them. The women were leaving men whose careers had stalled, whose dreams had come to not that much (which was worse than nothing)—these men directing community theater after hours, these men forced to let their rock and roll bands in rust-belt cities dissolve. The women left men who took them for granted, men who sometimes made huge plates of cheese and crackers and sat on the couch in their gym shorts watching police dramas.

Before the women left, they met their fellow women in bars and drank and took up smoking again and talked their decisions through.

"He's so cheap."

"He's always criticizing me."

"He thinks he's sensitive, but he's lost in his own world. I don't know how many times I've told him I don't like my ears licked during sex. It's like an oil spill lapping at my head."

"And you don't want his drool in your ear canal."

"And he still does it?"

"He says he gets lost in the moment."

"Time for him to get lost, all right."

"Can I say something? Tim is so *proud* of his cock. It's like, every time, we have to spend ten minutes just *looking* at it."

"That's why he bought that camera, Suzanne; he's going to shoot a photo essay."

The women laughed.

"I wish Steve would just accept what he's got and stop worrying about it. Seriously, I think that's why he's always so critical of me; it's like he's diverting attention from his little wiener."

The women paused to think briefly about their husbands' penises, feeling a confusing mix of desire, nostalgia, estrangement, revulsion. For some of the women, not talking about their husbands like this had been a point of respect and loyalty, and they were exhilarated and troubled by the line that had been crossed. A few regretted that the conversation had taken this turn.

"You know, I don't drive with Luke anymore. If we have to go somewhere together, I let him drive. I'm sick of hearing about it."

"And try talking to *him* about anything. If I bring up one little thing, he says I do it, too."

"Like what?"

"Well, if I tell him he's always criticizing me, he says that I criticize him. It's like living with Johnnie Cochran."

"It's like arguing with one of those plastic clowns you can't tip over."

The women stubbed out their cigarettes and hit the dance floor together as toughened gangs, nonchalantly casing the joint for the kind of man they didn't necessarily need but wouldn't mind finding. Back at the table, they talked about how their men made the bed smell, made the bathroom smell. Men smelled bad.

Yet the women often left men for other men. They snuck back into the sack with men from their college and graduate school days, old friends from when they felt a greater sense of possibility. The women were leaving men for men who seemed to have the ambition and the potential their husbands used to have. Or not. Sometimes it was clear to friends and family that the woman's new man was actually kind of a jerk, passing off the inability to hold a job as a sign of integrity, implying that borrowing money was beating the system at its own game. Some new men had children from other marriages to whom they were fathers in chest-thumping bursts; some were troubled users of prescription drugs.

The existence of children, of course, made everything more painful. Some of the abandoned men were bothered by the relief they felt when the women took the kids with them; other men anticipated fighting for split physical custody, if it came to that. A few of the women suggested that they would have no interest in being a primary custodial parent, that, in fact, the men could perform this role. The men accepted this possibility, in theory, yet it was surprisingly disconcerting to see women proposing major life decisions based on such new principles. In any case, the kids now represented something the men needed to salvage, to do right, and by doing right somehow show (and this made them cry at night, these men) that the women who left them were not the women they were promised if they did the right things and repudiated the Neanderthal crap of their fathers and their fathers' fathers.

On these emotional nights, the men reset the alarms on their digital clocks a few precious minutes later, hoping to regain by sleeping in some of what they were losing by lying awake in the dark on the old king-size bed. They turned over the pillows they had dampened with tears, and the new side of the pillows was cool and dry, like the forehead of, say, Chuck Yeager, the instant before ejecting from a test F-16 about to crash into the desert floor.

The wee hours certainly were a strange and superstitious time. But at work the next day, the men would forget about the self-indulgent crying, about what they would have called "despair" at 2:13 AM but referred to enigmatically as a "late night" at 10:00 AM in their brightly lit offices. And sometimes, then, on their lunch hours, a compensatory buoyancy would overtake the men as they drank invigorating Cokes with deli sandwiches and let their imaginations follow passing women. And every feeling, good or bad, was more intense than it had been in years.

The men also gathered in bars to discuss their departing women.

"I don't know what made her so dissatisfied."

"I've tried so hard not to say this, for so long, but she's a fucking bitch. I'm sick of caring about her feelings and what she *needs*."

"She's actually dating a biker?"

"Dude practically stabbed her in the chest with a broom handle—my kid told me."

"We would never do that."

"I hardly even ever yelled at her."

The women left the men because they could; the women left the men because they shouldn't. These women sometimes defied their mothers and siblings, who generally liked the abandoned men, men who shopped carefully for schools and insurance and didn't drink too much (or, if they once did, were in AA now, unlike their fathers, who never fessed up). Yes, these men looked good on paper. And yet many days on their way home from work, contemplating their tedious mates and their dead lives, these women had to pull into the parking lots of fast food restaurants and cry their eyes out. They called friends on their cell phones to get some support.

"I told him I need to *live!*"

"And what did he say?"

"He said, 'Isn't that what we're doing?' And I said, 'No!'"

"Good for you."

The men couldn't figure out exactly what was wrong. They thumbed the labels off their beer bottles and cautiously aired their flaws with each other, hoping to be excused.

"And so what if I went to *one* fucking porn site when she took Eleanor to Indianapolis for the weekend."

"This couple I know from work, Ann and Dave, they watch porn *together.*"

"Oh, Lordy."

"Hey, how'd she know you went to that site?"

"We've got this new HP where, as you're typing in a URL, it calls up past addresses your browser's been at."

"When did they start doing that?"

"Busted, dude."

"Fuck you."

"Better get a new computer, Chris."

"I said fuck you."

"You make *one* mistake. *One!*"

During tense family reunion dinners, after the women moved out but before anything had been decided, the men leapt up from the table to get the inevitable peanut butter and jelly supplement for little Emma's dinner or to refill a sippy cup. They used their napkins properly and swallowed their belches. *One mistake*, they thought. They chuckled mildly while their still-wives told funny stories about work to lighten the mood, to experiment mentally with whether they could be a family again.

And after the men did their best at those reunion dinners yet the women were unmoved, the men tried to keep their growing desperation under control.

"She's so stubborn. I knew the second she brought up possibly separating, she wasn't coming back. No matter what I did."

"My counselor said to give her all the space she needs. I shouldn't pressure her."

"My counselor said the same thing."

"So did mine."

"Piss me off."

"She *owes* me. I've done everything she's wanted me to."

"Probably not."

"You're right; I haven't."

The men laughed but it was not exactly funny.

Some of the men who were left by women started to look around their offices for sympathetic females; they raked their memories for women who had shown an interest but whom they'd had to avoid to safeguard the integrity of their marriages. Others turned to the stock market for companionship, researching and trading, watching the map of the market on Web sites. Some of the men resented all talk of the stock market because it reminded them that they had squat for savings, that they would need to rely on inheritances from their successful and stable fathers, fathers who for some reason had never had their women leave them. It didn't make sense, basically, for someone to fall out of love with you.

Some of the men couldn't help but think that the love was still there, that decades from now they would exchange knowing eye contact on the balcony of their time-share in the Bahamas, clink glasses with a smiling sigh, wonder what they had been thinking when their marriage almost blew up. When it was time to order new checks from the bank, these men placed the order with both names in the address corner.

As their hopes ebbed and flowed, the abandoned men swam through weeks of introspective limbo. They were not afraid of their feelings. They had constructed an emotional range they were proud of and could live within, yet they wondered if they weren't lying to themselves in the deepest ways. Some began to eat scary amounts or frequent gentlemen's clubs (at first, in groups, as a joke, a sort of collective "ah, get out of my face" to the women who had left them with so few stated reasons you could really believe, but then singly, in the middle of Saturday afternoons, wearing repressed quiet expressions that concealed the rage of self-loathing while women in g-strings performed demented gymnastic routines with chrome poles). Had they always been the unreconstructed men the progressive element of their society wanted to remake all along? This doubt gnawed at the men who had been left by the women. They said to themselves: "I always knew I was an asshole, and Valerie leaving just proves it."

The women who were leaving the men were flush with bravery

and sadness and desperation and new goals. The men began the difficult process of saving face, seizing on the sadness of their departing women as if it held a comforting explanation.

"She's depressed is the problem."

"I wanted her to get on something, but she wouldn't."

"She's so stubborn."

"I hate to say it, because I know how it'll sound, but deep down I know she's fooling herself."

"I worry more about her than about me," some men concluded. The others nodded. The men thought the women were damaged and reckless and headed for subsidized housing, God forbid, but they themselves were strong and sane. The women were crazy and quixotic, living out of self-help books and pining after phantasm men who didn't exist, while the men thought they had seen through to the smaller truths that made life feasible.

As things degenerated, the women wept on the phone with the men they were leaving one day, then refused to return calls for a week. Sometimes the women withheld their new addresses, as if their husbands were stalkers. Every man remembered the first time he left a message for the woman who was leaving him only to have that call returned by her lawyer.

But the worst thing was that no one pitied the men enough. They tried to pity each other, but they repelled each other. They couldn't just say "suck it up and be a man," because they had repudiated that attitude—yet their reward was not forthcoming.

Papers were always filed suddenly. The men tried to keep a grip. They programmed computers with morose expressions on their faces. They taught law school and made corrosive asides while explicating civil procedure, tempted by an ever-renewable supply of female students on which they could take their pleasure and their revenge—because they had worked so hard to be good, to be the men they were supposed to be instead of the men their fathers had been. And maybe this was why the women left them: their backward-looking dad obsession and its attendant corrosive sadness. (But if the women overheard this, they'd say, "So typical, thinking it's all about him. Blaming his poor dad. At least you knew who you were dealing with when you talked to his old man.")

The men were furious because, in the end, they hadn't been able to stop the women from leaving. They were upset when they realized everything their counselor had told them to do had made it easier for the women to go. The men passed into ruefulness. Then the men passed into watching football and cheering with abandon, until, as fourth quarters progressed, car commercials grew sad, no matter how tightly that Cadillac cornered.

But sometimes, in the eye of the hurricane of their rage and pain, the men found themselves breathing and in reasonably good health. They ate doughnuts and watched college basketball on TV and went drinking after work with whoever else stayed late—be it man or woman. Who had tricked them into marriage, into family life? Who said they had to love again? They could respectably decline the strain of intimacy like someone with high cholesterol turning down a pork chop. They could be like great ballplayers retiring at forty. At these times, not having to be in love—or to pretend they were in love—seemed an infinite vacation.

Meanwhile, the women leaving the men were worried and happy. They knew in their hearts they were right. They could be wrong, and it would be hard, but they knew in their hearts they were right.

The men had no persuasive answer to this. They simply watched the process of leaving. Late at night, they stood in dark hallways between their kitchens and downstairs bathrooms, feeling drafts from under back doors on their bare feet. Digital clocks on the kitchen counters marked minutes. As each minute prepared to flash instantaneously into the next, the men felt themselves on the brink of a startling insight.

Father Bob had the hots for their housekeeper. She was new. She was young. This was 1977.

But still he behaved like a model priest. His homilies bubbled with intensity, joy, brio. He soldiered extra hospital rounds, worked miracles in the confessional with a tough-to-execute tone of firm empathy. He took the lion's share of the late-night crisis calls: talking down the suicidal, finding safe haven for battered women, sending wayward husbands home. The alcoholics, the unemployed, the deranged—all the problem parishioners of Our Lady of Sorrows found a friend in Father Bob. He listened, he cut slack. He cut everyone slack, more slack than a priest who lusted after his housekeeper might need himself.

In his younger days, his conscience always had a way of finding out exactly what he feared doing most and then making him do it. Sell all you own and follow Me. Jesus said that. Give your life to Christ. You had to. So what he'd feared most as a conscience-ridden, masturbating, Pope John XXIII–admiring, Near South Side Chicago teenager was that God might ask him to become a priest. He knew he should because he was always wanting to fornicate, and being a priest was the best way to put a lid on that. He knew he should because too many of his friends were getting girls pregnant, driving drunk, gambling, stealing cars, buying prostitutes, lighting things on fire, defecating in Harrison Park, swearing at clergy, smoking reefer, fighting, skipping school, breaking windows, spray-painting El trains, denouncing God. He knew he should because the identity was ready-made and respectable and came with meals and clothes and housing and a grand purpose, and it would please his home-maker mother and his mortician father and the whole extended Lincheski clan no end.

And so he'd gone the seminary way. Where sex was mainly spo-ken of as something that would come between their future flocks and God, something they put aside because they were special—they were going to be *priests.* (He would never be a mere mister, or a dad, but a *Father,* as close to God as a man could get.) Instead of sex, there was the purgative way, which was a detaching of oneself not just from sex but from sweets, from alcohol, from cigarettes, from you name it; there was the contemplative way, the unitive way. He was going right up the spiritual ladder.

His rector at the sem had a hair shirt, a gag gift sent by an old friend who had veered into the Trappists. It was sleeveless, coarse, and scratchy, actually made of goat hair. The goat part intrigued Bob because weren't goats an emblem for sexual rambunctiousness? One night, during a rare social gathering in the rector's study, the young seminarians had stoked their virginal curiosity into a call for "the shirt," and the rector disappeared into his private quarters to retrieve the item. Bob touched it in his turn and immediately un-derstood the principle: each black, brown, or white hair was brittle enough to scratch and poke, and each hair extended at a slightly dif-ferent angle, so whenever you moved you were scratched, pricked, and stung differently, reminded that your Savior's body was a site of pain, taught that to be touched was excruciating.

The hair shirt also reminded Bob that, despite being on the purgative way, he couldn't go more than three days between masturbation sessions. He felt compelled to bring this up with the rector, no matter the embarrassment, to get some encouragement in facing his weakness. He hung around after his fellow seminarians had turned in, helping the rector tidy up.

The rector was a laconic, pipe-smoking, moderate-drinking, silver-haired man, tall, with pointy shoulder bones set so far apart that it seemed his chest was a sail. He had his long fingers down the necks of about six beer bottles, carrying them through the hallway to a little kitchen, where a dim light burned. Bob trailed behind, a bottle in each hand.

"I know we're a secular order, Father, but that hair shirt's not a bad idea."

The rector put the bottles on the counter, removing his fingers, then rinsed them, one by one, in the sink.

"To be honest, Bob, I don't wear it. But you're welcome to try it."

"I think I might," Bob said. "I think I need something to get me focused, Father. I'm having trouble . . . I can't purge as much as I should. Certain things are always on my mind. Not *always*, but—"

"Don't be discouraged," the rector said blandly. "Think of it as a cross." Drying his hands, he let his eyes meet Bob's, managed to make his words more than just boilerplate advice; recognition, almost an admission, flickered there.

What an idea! A cross that could bring him closer to God! His desire to jerk off was really a type of suffering. Each time he did, it was like Jesus falling down on the way to Calvary. This cross hadn't been easy to bear, but he'd carried it right into his assistant's position at Our Lady of Sorrows.

Then this housekeeper. Barbara Fuller. This housekeeper. The rectory had never had a housekeeper born after World War I. There had been a series of ageless Polish and German and Puerto Rican widows with tremendous forearms who treated the priests as if they were ten-year-old sons. Barbara Fuller was a problem. She was in the building. He desired her. He would retire to his room and pollute himself to *Charlie's Angels* with the sound off on the little black and white his mother had given him because she was worried the holy man wouldn't have his feet on the ground. (Now he understood why there'd been no TV and no radio at the sem.) After two months of Ms. Fuller, he was feeling reckless and giddy.

She came from the North Shore. This in itself was mysterious. What was a young woman—no more than twenty-seven—from Evanston doing answering a want ad in a church bulletin from Logan Square? It was scary, how she'd materialized in his life, almost as if his sexual thoughts had conjured her. Mrs. Hetzel, the secretary, had hired her, but by chance Father Bob was in the office that day. Barb was sincere and pretty, though a little pale, as if she'd just gotten over a bad flu. Her two front teeth pressed together, making a tooth tepee at the entrance to her mouth. Her long dark hair was parted in the middle and feathered on the sides, like Jaclyn Smith. A nice figure. It was all there: she was a woman. The tooth thing was very cute. He had met women who were more attractive, but none of them straightened his room, did his laundry, changed the sheets on his bed.

She came by Mondays, Wednesdays, and Fridays, between noon and three-thirty, when Bob usually was doing rounds at St. Elizabeth's or teaching a religion class at the grade school (he told the kids not to worry about hell, told them the devil was only a symbol). He found himself rushing home for a glimpse of her on her way out. He prewashed his underwear in the bathroom sink, collected his hairs from toilet and tub. Should he leave his clothes on the floor for her to pick up? This made her seem like his wife. Or should he put everything in the hamper to show what a neat guy he was? He decided to be moderately messy: he wanted to engage her cleaning attention without being a pain in the ass. He left *The Electric Kool-Aid Acid Test* on his nightstand to prove he was no square, periodically advancing the bookmark until he'd "finished" it. This was about the time he suspected he was in love with her.

Home early from the hospital one afternoon, he caught up with her near the dryer in the basement. "So, how's it going?" he asked.

"Fine," she said. "How'm I doing?"

"Fine, great. I've heard no complaints."

"Well, I'm glad I'm here. I mean, I'm glad you're letting me do this." She talked a little louder than most people.

"You like to clean?" he asked neutrally. There was possibility for insult either way.

"I'm really a photographer," she said. "Or I'm supposed to be."

"I'm sorry, I never thought to ask you—"

"That's all right. You probably thought I was some dumb housewife bored out of my skull."

"No, not at all. I try not to pry too much."

"You just wait for it in the confessional."

"I love confessions."

"Father!"

He smiled, as if to say, "You asked for it." Was she flirting with him? He realized *he* was flirting with her. In his excitement, he hiccuped. "Excuse me," he said.

"Far out!" she said. "I've never heard a priest hiccup."

"I'm not supposed to," he said, feeling strange, light-headed. Now he'd done it: shown her he had a body. The hiccups were coming about every ten seconds.

"I'm sorry," Barb said. "I'm making you self-conscious. You should put your head in a paper bag or something. I'll go get one."

"No, it's OK. You're doing great," he managed to say, between hiccups. "I'm going upstairs now."

"All right. Well, thanks, Father. I'm glad it's working out. God knows nothing else in my life is." She laughed.

Bob looked back at her. "Something wrong?" The idea of her bringing him her problems gave him stirrings.

She bent over and took an armful of clothes out of the dryer. "See you around," she called out, as if she hadn't heard him.

* * *

They saw each other often. School let out and Bob had an extra afternoon free. He had a scenario: circumstances call away Father Joe and Father Miguel; she works late, gets sweaty, a shower, his touch . . . The fantasy seemed tantalizingly within reach. He kept tabs on his compadres' schedules, thought of excuses to keep her late. But he enacted nothing, never made advances. Before leaving the seminary, he'd actually gotten his own hair shirt, mail-ordered from an outfit that specialized in ecclesiastical knickknacks, and now he took to wearing it again. Though it reminded him of a welcome mat (it was dyed the same rusty-brown color), some of the old spiritual devotion inhered in its bristling strands, and it steadied him for a bit. But its power had recently suffered a devastating blow when *Charlie's Angels* had driven him to masturbate—*while wearing the shirt.*

In his less libidinous moods, he thought about the rest of his life. Staying celibate for the next fifty years or leaving the priesthood: both scared him. His hugs would get squeezier; people would whisper about him; somebody would catch him, a fifty-, a sixty-, a seventy-year-old priest, exposing himself to passing El trains; propositioning Girl Scouts; pulling his pud in the vestry, in the john in the church basement, in the woods on a retreat. A life of surreptitious gratification depressed him. But if he left the priesthood, how would he make a living? And wouldn't it be terrible to betray God just because he was horny? Besides, Barb intimidated him: she could be sharp-sounding, and there was something knowing in her laugh, which could get maniacal.

Yet she began putting herself in his path more and more, apparently working longer so he would run into her even if he was late getting home. Occasionally they talked. She seemed to believe in sin, heaven and hell, which made him doubt she was "loose"; he was almost happy to learn she was divorced. She told him several times that she didn't know what to do with her life. She photographed weddings and did other commercial work, but she wasn't "fulfilled" (her word). Father Bob nodded solemnly as he listened.

Then one afternoon she asked him if he wanted to meet her for a cup of coffee at a place up in Evanston, for a friendly chat, she said.

Bob said yes without thinking. His heart felt kicked into the air. He tried to look into her eyes with great, loving significance, but her eyes slipped his.

* * *

He took the Fullerton bus to the Howard El and on up into Evanston, then got off at Dempster. The coffee shop was just east of the tracks. He wore mufti, brown Haggar slacks and a white button-down shirt. But he kept the black shoes of his habit, telling himself half-facetiously that they would keep him morally grounded. He was very clean, brushed, shaved, flossed, deodorized. He had Listerined his mouth, slipped fresh Odor Eaters into his shoes. There was no wax in his ears, no snot in his nose. His bladder and bowels had been nervous all day; he was dramatically empty of waste. He had examined himself naked in the mirror: thirty-four years old, soft but not yet fat. A hairy chest, broad enough shoulders. He rigged two mirrors to see himself from behind. He'd never seen himself this way. It was unnerving.

The operating fantasy was that this was a date; he would act this fantasy until he met resistance or until, probably, at some decisive last moment, he would pull up. He didn't want to dwell too much on the pulling-up part; the point was to go with the fantasy as long as possible. These days, he knew, sex not only happened on first dates, it happened before dates had even been scheduled, within hours, even minutes, of meeting. The two condoms in his wallet attested to his seriousness (two, in case he botched one—tore it, dropped it, lost it, who knew what could happen); he thought of them, oddly, as a pair of poker chips, his stake. He did want her, he did. But he also carried what he considered to be the suppressed, blasphemous hope of Abraham as he took unwitting Isaac up Mt. Moriah: that he was being led to a sacrifice but at the last minute an unexpected reprieve would manifest itself.

Now he stepped into the coffee shop. She sat by a brick wall and waved to him. He waved back and grinned. Once this expression took over his face, it was hard to get rid of. Crossing the crowded, smoky room, stepping sideways to pass between two hard wooden chairs, he rubbed the corners of his mouth to erase it, the grin.

"Thanks for coming, Father Bob," she said.

"Bob. Just Bob."

He didn't want any coffee at the moment. She sipped hers.

"I suppose you're wondering why we're meeting like this," she said.

"No. I mean, I thought we could meet . . . like this."

"That's good. That makes me happy. I don't want you feeling weird or anything." She fitted a cigarette to her mouth. A clear gloss coated her lips. He couldn't decide whether it was lipstick or a balm. The distinction seemed to make a difference. She was wearing jeans and a white, sleeveless blouse that buttoned in front.

"I don't have matches," he said, half to himself.

She produced a lighter, lit up. They small-talked for a bit—his El ride, his civilian duds.

"Can I ask you a question?" she said, and she puffed. "This just occurred to me. Do you mind if it's, you know, personal?"

"No, ask me anything."

"*Anything?*" She made a show of stroking her chin, about to ask the ultimate question, then shook the pose with a laugh. "No, I just wanted to know why you became a priest. Is that too private?"

"Privacy schmivacy," he said, and he smiled in a goofy way. He had wanted to say, musingly, "Actually, I've been thinking about that lately," to open the subject of his commitment to his vocation, but it felt too disingenuous. "Well," he tried, "I've always had a thing with my conscience, with God, and . . . it's hard to explain. I think I liked the idea of being nice to people all the time." He burst out with embarrassed laughter. "Being a priest helps you be nice, because everyone's always looking at you." He was stunned by how stupid he sounded.

"So, no flashing light? I mean, the heavens didn't open up?"

"Not even a smoky shrub." He chortled woodenly. He wanted to tell her that for people with spiritualities like his own, it wasn't so clear. No light, no drama, just your conscience doing its constant work. But he didn't want to bore her or seem too serious.

"Yeah, well, I wish I'd been a nun."

"Hey, it's never too late."

"It is, Father. It's *way* too late. My life's been a total mess."

"Nobody's perfect," he said foolishly. "Where'd you grow up?"

"Wilmette," she said, as if this summed up everything. "My father was a partner in Beaumont and Sullivan—it's like the biggest law firm *in the world.* And he was a drunk. So's my mom. She beat us kids with her hairbrush, but we took great family vacations!" She laughed convulsively.

He gave her the old compassionate look.

"My objective in life was not to give a shit. When I was fifteen, my friends turned me on to pills. You should've seen us, white lipstick, tons of black eye shadow—we looked like vampires." She laughed again, pleased with herself. "I should've headed for the nunnery right then, Father, but I ran away to Miami."

Another minute and it was clear she was bent on telling him the whole story. He could not choose but to hear: how she had tried to find the sympathetic desk clerk from the Bal Harbour Hotel with whom she'd flirted on vacation; how from a pay phone on Highway 1 she called the number he'd given her a year before and got a woman who said *Lo siento* and hung up; how she eventually moved in with Astro the dealer and was planning to defect to Cuba before her father finally caught up with her on a tip from a nurse at the free clinic.

"I'm sorry," she said. "Is this boring you?"

"What, are you kidding?" He was feeling more comfortable now.

"Father," she said, half-scolding, half-bemused. She crushed out her cigarette. "But don't you get sick of it, everyone's dirty laundry?"

"I *like* dirty laundry."

"Bob, please."

He grinned mildly.

She studied his face. "Do you by any chance smoke pot?"

"I never have," he said. But then he remembered he had a few times, before the sem. Still, he didn't want to blow his cover.

"Would you?"

"Why not?"

"I live about three blocks away. Can you deal with it?"

The question, as a question, really didn't register with Bob. He just knew that he was going to go to where she lived.

As they walked back under the El, she told him how much she had loved her father, who had passed away just a year ago. She told how her dad wanted to make mulberry wine one fall, and she and her brother and sister stomped mulberries for him in the backyard. She kept repeating how they stomped and stomped those mulberries, as if she couldn't convey how great it was. "Because, you know, *we were making Dad's wine!*"

"Yeah," Bob said.

There was a pause when they reached the door to her building. Bob noticed two last names on her mailbox—the second, "Fitzgerald," hand-lettered above the typed "Fuller." He followed her up the creaking, carpeted stairs. "My roommate's visiting her folks in Wisconsin," she called back, as if she knew he had seen the names.

She let him into a medium-sized apartment. The furniture was all wood and pillows and futony things; a lot of plants; a large, six-sided fish tank; a stereo and maybe three hundred albums in old apple crates; paintings on the walls with too much color and confusion; fewer photographs than he had expected.

Then she turned to him as if something had just occurred to her. "Is this freaking you out? I mean, do priests *go* to people's apartments?"

"I'm fine," he said, looking around with his hands in his pockets. He had chills; his underarms were sweating; his deodorant had given up.

"Do you want something to drink?"

"Sure."

"Whoa, Father Bob means it. How about a gin and tonic? We've got shitloads of gin."

"Yeah, that's great."

She brought the drinks, set them on a low table between two large white candles, which she then lit, along with several others on shelves around the dim room. The air filled with the cloying smells of vanilla and cinnamon. "I love candles. Emily, my best friend in the world, she makes candles. God, I have to tell you about Emily. One more thing." She pulled a tin of Sucrets out of a desk drawer, sat cross-legged in an armchair, slipped back into her story.

By sixteen, she was on the loose again, hitching to Tijuana with her boyfriend, whom she married before a Mexican JOP, high on tequila and cough medicine. She spent her honeymoon in the backseat of an ancient Packard in a used-car lot. They set up house in Oceanside, until one day she came home to find Ben shooting up heroin in the living room with his friends. "My husband!" Barb exclaimed, still incredulous. "I hit the ceiling: 'Junkies outta my house!' He said, 'It's not your house, babe. It's mine.' He took me to the bedroom, closed the door, and beat the living hell out of me. And I . . . next thing I remember was being outside the front door with my stuff in a backpack.

"A real asshole," she added. "By the way, do you want another drink?"

"I *need* another drink."

"No kidding." She took his glass. "I get like this. I talk and I can't stop. Am I being selfish?"

"Of course not."

She did a double take, smiled. "All right. Let's get you that drink. Then we can smoke a joint."

Bob asked if he could use the bathroom. On his way back to the living room, he glanced into one of the bedrooms. It was already dusk, so he could just make out a desk, bookshelves, a butterfly chair, some photography equipment—but no bed. The door to the other bedroom at the end of the hall was nearly closed. He fairly staggered at the possibility: did she sleep with her roommate? Was she a lesbian? But she'd been married. Maybe her terrible relationships with men drove her to this. Disappointment and relief washed through him in successive waves. What was he doing here? What was this all about?

They sat down again with new drinks. Barb pulled a joint from the Sucrets tin, lit it, inhaled, passed it to Bob. His first sip of smoke tripped sharply against his throat. After his coughing settled down, he said, "At least I didn't get the hiccups."

As she set off again, Bob felt himself drifting back to his job, back to being a priest with another problem parishioner unspooling the misery. He hadn't really thought about her character before, but now that he'd heard a good deal about her life she seemed, well, screwed up. Her friendliness, her proximity, her femaleness—these were the things he liked about her, and these worldly things had somehow sent him so far from his life's purpose. Yet none of this really mattered because (despite the hugs, the tearful counseling sessions, the embarrassing "thank you" notes) all of his previous relationships were just the shadows of real relationships, and that's how this would end up, too. Priests, psychiatrists, prostitutes—*c'est la même chose*, as his compadre Hying at the sem was fond of saying: professional friends. He would never be of the people, and he would never be a saint.

The joint went back and forth. Bob watched Barb's mouth intently, as if the movements of her lips themselves were saying something other than her words. He gathered she was now living on a houseboat with swordfishermen. She laughed at something, something at her mother's expense. He liked her laugh, though it *was* maniacal.

"Are you all right, Father?"

"I'm feeling a lot, if that's what you mean." The alcohol and the pot were working miracles together. He wanted to lick her teeth; he wanted to touch where she had been talking, to suck on her tongue, which worded her character. Maybe her lesbian relationship only showed a taste for sexual adventure. He imagined her naked. He imagined chasing her past the fish tank. He was much nicer than Astro, or the swordfishermen, or the heroin husband. She would fight him off, or she would fellate him. He held the joint with trembling fingers, pondered it, toked on it.

He could hardly pay attention now, getting only glimpses of the good times with Emily in the hills above Monterey, of her brief college days in Colorado, of her living with her new boyfriend in the desert, dealing full-time, turning over a thousand pounds of pot a week. Something about brown Mexican heroin and diabetics' needles and her husband—at some point she'd gotten married again—firing a warning shot at her one afternoon with his gun. Then some other day he's dragging her through the living room by the hair. She snaps, gets the gun, misfires it at him, and proceeds to stalk him through the house. Bob's attention came straggling back.

She can't believe what she's doing, gives the gun over to Ted. They try to talk things out, but Barb knows he's bullshitting. Her actual mouth was talking: "I told him, 'Let me put the gun away. If you trust me, you'll let me put the gun away.' And he hands me the gun and he hands me the clip and I put the clip back in the gun and I fire two shots and I killed him."

She stared at him, her lips quivering, eyes brimming with tears. He kept losing his focus on her, kept having to re-establish his understanding of her face, who she was, why he was there. She went out of focus as Barb and came back into focus as a killer. Isaac had been killed, after all. But then the killer became Barb, too, the person he'd been talking to, who laughed loudly and cleaned his room and loved her dead father. Barb had killed a man, and he, Bob, had heard yet another confession. It was unbelievably sad. This was probably her entire purpose in asking him for coffee, in showing up at the rectory far from the people who knew her on the North Shore.

"Can I have it?" she asked.

"Have what?"

"Absolution."

The word came at him like a fragment of someone else's memory. His priestliness seemed on the fritz, shorted out by despair and a lust that was like a conflict of interest. "I don't think I can do it right now," he heard himself say.

She looked at him, wiped her wet eyes.

"You don't want it from me," he tried to explain. He smiled weakly, as if he were a notorious absolution bungler, his many dissatisfied customers frying in hell. But why couldn't he at least go through the motions for her? Maybe he had never really had a vocation; maybe he had trusted the sting of masochism instead of waiting for the shock of the light.

"I got off on temporary insanity," Barb said. Her voice was breaking. "I feel that way. I'm still insane sometimes." The way she said it made it sound like the main reason she needed absolution.

"You're OK," he said. He mustered a fit of slack-cutting. "You were really suffering. You couldn't let it go on that way."

"I killed him," she said miserably, and she wept.

He made an instinctive move toward her, scooting to the edge of the futon couch. She noticed this and came toward him, too, and they stood up and hugged each other. Bob had never been hugged so hard. His entire body seemed to wake up. Then she staggered away from him and blew her nose.

"I need another drink," she said. "You?"

"No, let's not," he said. He wanted to hug her again, to console her more, because the enormity of what had happened to her kept blooming in his mind, but he also still wanted her, which was another reason to hug her, and yet the two reasons somehow canceled each other out, which was maddening.

"You must be pissed at me for bringing you up here for this," she said.

"Like water off a duck." He waved a wobbly hand.

"What did you think this was going to be, anyway?"

"I didn't know," Bob said. "Maybe drinks, massages, stuff like that."

"You're a priest."

"That's just a front. What I am is, I'm a lover."

She considered him, seemed to control her expression. Was she about to laugh?

"Nope," she said. "Sorry." Her voice was cracking again. She shook her hair off her forehead. "I don't want to be the one to bring you down," she added in a quiet voice. "I already brought one man down." But she looked him in the eye; it was like being hooked up to a lie detector.

"I'm already down," Bob said. "I'm like you. I like you because I'm like you."

"I'm a mess."

"*I'm* a mess. Two wrongs make a right."

"Bob, you're talking nutty," she said, but more of her smile came back.

He moved toward her. He had no idea what he was doing, but he knew that it had started with and would continue with her mouth (the Word made flesh, he couldn't help but think), and once he was connected to her mouth, she would tell him what to do. So he kissed her mouth, and it opened for him.

"We're OK, right?" she said under her breath, between kisses.

He wanted to say something light or witty or even seductive, but he also wanted to answer her with something true, except he wasn't sure how to say something true about what they were doing. He found himself nodding, though she didn't seem to notice.

She directed the undressing, guided him to the couch, folded herself under him.

"When should I put the rubber on?" he asked.

"Now would be a good time," Barb said.

And then Bob did what he had wanted to do every single day since he was fourteen. He didn't do it with much finesse or for very long, but he did it.

Afterward, they lay together on the futon couch.

"Did we just do that?" Barb asked, and she laughed a little to herself.

Bob smiled, feeling strange and giddy, as though they were both suspended high in the air, but then he realized Barb was tearing up again.

Her emotion surprised him. He'd been so caught up in what this would mean to himself that he'd never really thought of what it might mean to her. "I'm sorry," he said. "I'm so sorry. I shouldn't have—"

"No, it's OK. I just get really emotional sometimes." She rubbed the corner of each eye with the heel of her hand. "Come here, Mr. Bob."

She moved into his body and they hugged each other, a hug that Barb didn't seem to want to end. Though the position of his neck and shoulders was very awkward, Bob kept holding on.

After she released him, she went on to describe her trial. This was part of what had to be told—Bob should have known. He lay on his right side, listening, with his right arm stretched straight over his head, the knot of his shoulder a sort of pillow. It reminded him of high school, before he transferred to the sem, how he and his buddies would raise their hands emphatically in class and then give long, wildly incorrect answers to throw off the teacher. It was strange to realize that this was the same arm he'd had back then.

And this was the body Barb had had all that time—the feet that had stomped the mulberries, the forearms that blocked her mother's hairbrush and her husbands' fists, the breasts that had been caressed by other men, perhaps other women, the hands that had held the gun. The tooth tepee itself was probably a sign of her runaway days, the problem likely developing during all those years without dental appointments. He watched her face as she talked, and he thought of her naked body not as the tempting flesh that covered her bedraggled soul but as the physical site of her life. Her body carried all of her past with it, just as his body carried all of his.

They started kissing again, but it felt different now. She took him into the bedroom.

"Your roommate?" he asked, belatedly overcome with adulterous guilt.

"Katie? Like I said, she's in Wisconsin."

"I know, but there's only one bed."

"Oh, you priests have the dirtiest minds. She's just crashing here for a while—her husband is insane."

This time she lay on her side, but with her shoulders almost flat on the pillow. She guided Bob into her from behind, her left leg awkwardly raised while Bob, like a gentleman, helped her hold it up. She explained that this angle was easier on her urethra, so she wouldn't get a bladder infection as she sometimes did when she drank and had sex—besides, she said with a laugh, it was a good position for "helping myself out." Bob couldn't believe that she could talk about her body like this, that she might masturbate while they did it.

She told him that it worked best for her if he went slowly or held still altogether. Her head was on the pillow with her hair spread around. There was candlelight, of course. She told him to start moving a little more, and he was pleased to obey. She was getting close, trembling. Her eyes were closed but concentrating on what she was doing. She was with him, but he was forgotten. Her mouth was open. Those teeth. Her hand moved more quickly. Her face. There was plain sincerity in her quiet noises, in the look on her face as she came. There was no flash of light, only the look on her face. He never expected it. He never thought anything could be so lovely. And he defied anyone or anything to mess with it.

Take this: Daddy was a trucker. One night when we sat on the picnic table holding sparklers in our hands, he told me he liked trucking on account of how the road felt beneath you.

"You ever stand at the top of a staircase, Little Bugger?"

I nodded.

"Then you know what I'm talking about."

The long fleshy sparks flew, but nothing started on fire.

* * *

Then, years later, Daddy took off his hat. His gray and black hair stuck to his head in curly waves like worn-out shag carpeting.

"Did you ever vacuum your hair?" I asked him.

"No, not right now."

"I said did you ever. I did. A couple times."

"What? No, I won't do it."

"Today at school we had confession. Do you want to know what I confessed?" I had it in mind to tell him about the various items I'd stolen that week from the warehouse food outlet—jumbo bags of M&M's, a cigarette lighter, a copy of *Heavy Metal* magazine—and how I sometimes had some cigarettes and alcohol and hashish, and how I was drawing pictures of naked girls on the sidewalk, in the snow, on my hand, on the rubber tip of my tennis shoes, on mail-boxes, on bathroom stalls.

"Don't come to me with your goddamn confessions," he said, shaking his carpethead. "Don't confess to anyone. Don't ever think you've done something wrong. Well, sure, there's right and wrong and everything, but don't you ever confess to anybody. It's nobody's damn business but your own!"

We were standing there waiting for the bus, which we had run to catch but missed. The VW was in for repairs that whole winter.

* * *

Daddy was off the road for a few days and brought Momma home drunk on a summer night. They barreled up the gravel drive in Dad-dy's VW bus, slammed on the brakes, and skidded so that the front bumper tagged the garage door. I couldn't sleep anyway. I slipped to the living room and watched them through the window.

"I dare you!" Momma said, hard and disbelieving and drunk.

"All right. Fine," Daddy said.

That's when Daddy lunged across the front seat and flattened her against the door. She screamed, "Leon! Leeeeeon!" But Daddy was stronger. He pushed her out the door and reversed the bus into the street. Momma lay in the gravel in a cloud of gray dust. The yard lamp made the dust look more solid than it was. Daddy screeched down the road.

"I hope that bitch rots in hell," Momma said. She threw a fist-ful of stones down the driveway, crying. Then she lay back on the gravel. I walked outside carefully. I carried a blanket, a glass of or-ange juice, and a pillow. Her eyes opened up suddenly but slowly, like Frankenstein's.

"I brought you some juice," I said, putting the pillow under her fancy wig.

She closed her eyes. "Cut it off," she said. "Do it now when you don't care."

* * *

I went hunting with my daddy. We sat up in the tree fort with our bows and arrows, and I wore an orange wool hat with earflaps. The sky was one gray blanket. There were bare quiet trees and the smell of wood smoke. The leaves were right on the ground. I kept imagining the leaves rising back to the branches and greening again, then browning and falling. I raised them and let them fall, over and over, and then a tender doe strolled by. Somebody had already shot a doe on our party permit. Daddy fitted an arrow and drew it back, pointing his tongue out of the side of his mouth. But he didn't shoot. Daddy did not shoot. He didn't. Also, he thought compound bows were for sissies.

A week after the hunting trip, I had to go to the eye doctor with Momma. In the waiting room, Momma's hands were folded on her dress. They were small reddish hands with white joints. The dress was a little girl's dress with white and green flowers on a yellow background. But the cloth was all faded by the sun and her wearing it.

"I can see each thread in your dress."

"I'm getting pretty old, aren't I?"

So then we didn't talk.

It seemed the eye doctor took out my eyes and put back different ones because when we got home, Daddy had gone and every place I ever knew was changed. The rug by his chair where he left his empties was a ghost town of beer bottles. It wasn't like it was when he was just on the road. The sense of gone was pretty strong.

Too bad for us.

But it was a week until the light burned out in the hall outside my room.

I didn't tell Momma about the blackout because I thought light-bulbs cost a lot of money.

I'd come home after spending the day swearing at my teachers, marking the hallways with crayons, detonating toilet bowls with M-8os, breaking bottles, and exploring sewer tunnels. It'd be getting dark already. The hall light wouldn't work. In my room, I'd forget about everybody I ever knew. I wouldn't turn on the light in that room either. I'd just lie on the bed and stare at the dark Pittsburgh Steelers pennant on the wall, or look at the bare trees outside and listen to the big old window rattle.

One night, when I went to sleep, I dreamed Daddy came home. In my dream, I was younger, and the door opened by itself. He walked up slowly, rubbing his big hands together. I could barely smell die-sel. He breathed through his mouth because of his bad asthma. The light from outside lit his face. He had a beard to go with his mus-tache, but it was still him. When he noticed me watching him, he snorted like a spooked deer. But he came over and put his hand on my shoulder. He kissed the top of my head. I didn't want to move, I was so happy, and I told him it was great to see him and asked him where he'd been. He shushed me and told me we were going to shoot skeet at the club tomorrow. We could talk about everything then.

Later that night, I woke up from the dream about him coming home, and the dream seemed real. I crept down the dark hallway to the converted porch. I asked Momma where Daddy was because I couldn't wait for the skeet range.

Momma was watching one of those Cary Grant movies, about to start bleating like a fawn herself over Mr. Grant's looks and his ways.

"I'm just watching the TV," she said softly, fixed on the screen. "Don't be cruel. Your daddy's not coming home."

So then I knew I had just been dreaming about him. Maybe she was dreaming about him, too.

* * *

Things got to the point that when Momma made soup she'd say, "You carrots have had it" or "Potatoes—damn!" or "Come on now, celery!" and then her cleaver would come down and bounce the vegetable in half.

One time she set down the knife's warm handle. "What good are these rotten things?" she said. "Let's bury them."

So I got the shovel out of the garage. My pants had brown knees. I started to dig near Daddy's old compost pit.

"Over here," Momma corrected me. She held her wig in her hands out of respect.

* * *

One night we were watching the local TV station. They were showing Charlton Heston in *Ben Hur*. Mr. Heston drove his chariot and those fast horses straight into dangerous adventures fit for men. It was very competitive on that track. Metal blades rotated on the wheels of one of Mr. Heston's evil rivals. I tried to make a joke.

"That's what Daddy used to contend with on the open highway. Have mercy on him."

Momma cried.

A commercial came on right in the middle of the chariot race. The ad was for custom cakes made in the shape of things—a race car, a cougar, a human head. According to the woman on TV, a cake could be made "for any occasion!"

Momma said real slowly, "We're going to get some cake mixes and some ingredients and we're gonna bake and mold ourselves a life-size cake of your departed daddy."

"Momma, first we got to see if Daddy wins on the TV."

"That's not your daddy," she snapped. "That man and Chuck Heston don't have these two fingers in common."

She raised her pinkie on each hand and showed them to me.

"That's some discrepancy," she said.

Without even watching the rest of the movie, we went to the warehouse food outlet and bought seven yellow cake mixes and eleven chocolate cake mixes and two angel food cake mixes and four cartons of eggs and two bags of powdered sugar.

I was in charge of getting the frosting ready while Momma mixed the cake batter. The window was a mirror, reflecting our images: Momma working her spatula with a scrape and slap motion and me scooping yellows from one half of the eggshell to the other, letting the whites slip away into an old peanut butter jar. The mixer buzzed like a tiny airplane engine. Momma said, "Grease and flour those pans" or "Check the oven," but otherwise we didn't talk. When I put a toothpick in the first cake and it came out dry, I broke into a sweat and got chills all over.

When Momma pulled the last two cake pans out of the oven and set them on the stove, her face sagged like a sinkhole, her shoulders hunched, her eyes pressed out worms of tears. I went to hug her, but before I got there she yelled, "Holy Mary, Mother of God!" The way her cheeks quivered made me think of mice running under a blanket.

"It's OK," I said. But I held back from touching her, as if she was on fire.

We built the body on two card tables set up on the side of the kitchen. Momma made the neck a little too thin and it kept crumbling under her fingers. She reinforced it with frosting. I used red, yellow, and blue food coloring in the frosting for Daddy's body. I made his face red, his arms blue, his feet yellow, and the rest of him a mix of colors that turned out to be brown. By the time the sun was up, we had all of him there.

Momma didn't get one minute of sleep; she was off to her job at the Department of Transportation. When I took off for school, I left my tuna sandwich sitting next to Daddy's hand. "I hope you like it," I said. "I feel like stealing my lunch today."

At recess I told a few good friends that my daddy was a cake. After school I went out and threw rocks at trucks on the freeway with my friend Willy Newt. One sharp toss hit a windshield, and the trucker pulled over and chased us into the woods. Willy lost his footing when the turf clumps at the edge of the creek gave way, and he splashed into the water. When he climbed back on land he didn't have his glasses. His eyes were slits and his face looked puffy and splotched with pink. He tried to run but caught a branch across his face.

"I can't see," he said, almost crying. He dropped back into the brown water, feeling around for his glasses.

I stood and watched. The trucker finally came through the trees and told us the police were waiting.

Luckily Momma was at work, so she didn't get the call from the police—we were so scared we gave them the right phone numbers. Then Momma came home, but no one called. Still, I knew they were going to call back eventually, and Momma learning of my arrest was on my mind like a bag of rocks.

We had a regular meal of chicken, baked potatoes, and corn that left thick oily circles around our mouths. My greasy fingertips made the grip on my tall milk glass a little unsure.

Daddy was dessert. Momma peeled the plastic wrap off his body, pulling off gobs of frosting skin.

"Your daddy was mostly a tormented man," she said seriously. "I guess I was a part of that torment at times, with the way I would nag him on occasion and carry on." Momma stopped and squinted at her cleaver. I couldn't see her voice, but when I heard it again, it sounded like she'd just dipped it in feeling. Her voice was wet with it. "If you love something, set it free—that's what they all say. And just you watch, he'll go free. As free as I-70 can make a man." She picked up the cleaver and pulled herself together. She sighed. "In a way we're both failures because of what happened between us, only I'm left here to be a failure on the same failing ground while your daddy has escaped to greener pastures."

The whole idea of failure seemed to come from nowhere, but once it was in the room, it roosted on my young head.

Momma went on. "I've thought long and hard on this matter, and I think it's best to forgive him and get on with our lives as best we can."

I refilled my milk glass to have something to do. I stared at the *CBS Evening News with Dan Rather.* Meanwhile, Momma brought down her two-inch cleaver, taking a big portion out of Daddy's upper thigh. As Momma put the cake in front of me, I met Dan Rather's eyes. Dan Rather was a man; he knew how to behave. He looked the American People right in the eye. I thought Momma was going to say something any second, something like, "Dan Rather is a very impressive man." And I wouldn't have minded it one bit. But Momma was as silent as my daddy lying belly up on those card tables.

The phone didn't ring. I ate some Daddy. He tasted sweet and good.

When I went to bed, the police still hadn't called. I lifted open my window, hearing the counterweights slide inside the frame, and stood looking out. The cool air came up to me like an invisible wave of water. The moon was just getting started, and the naked trees were swaying but stiff, like old people trying to dance. Then I heard the back door open and shut and saw Momma in the yard, in her white gown and fuzzy slippers, stepping through the dark and over the ground. She pulled a short-handled spade from the folds of her gown. She threw her wig down, set her fuzzy slippers a working distance apart, and drove the spade into the cold earth. I heard the soft scratch of metal on fine pebbles. The wind was strong like a river, but the slippers gave no ground. She planted the spade again, using a foot for emphasis. She bent up the earth and shoveled the earth aside. She dug more. Then she set the spade in the grass and reached into her bosoms and pulled out a glowing crumbling thing that she spilled into the ground, pinching the stray crumbs with her fingers and tucking them under. She put the dirt back and patted it with her hands. From inside my stomach, the sugar from Daddy made me restless.

"Daddy was a good man," I said to myself. "May he rest in peace.

And may I turn out normal. May I someday anchor the *CBS Evening News with Stanton Muldowny*—if that's what it takes. May the demons that go around my head turn out to be friendly ghosts; may the everlasting life promised us if we are pretty good not turn out to be a hoax. May I not wake up one morning with my wife lying dutifully by my side, but with the only notion inside me being the following: I think there's something wrong with me, and so this day I pack myself and take myself with me, to find out just what the wrong thing is, in the hopes of fixing it . . . no matter what the cost . . . until death do us part . . . amen."

Right as I finished my prayer, Momma started back to the porch. Looking out at Daddy's grave, I walked two fingers like a hooded man to the middle of the windowsill and stood him beneath the heavy window hung from its frame by chains like a guillotine.

Kelly liked hair because each strand was thin and because you could cut a hundred hairs with one snip of the scissors. And then you could cut more. You saw the difference right away. The face showed more. The head seemed lighter, *was* lighter, without the cut hair. Which was gone. You could always win against hair. You could always cut it faster than it could grow.

Kelly was cutting Michelle's hair. Michelle wanted her hair short, well off her neck, more like Kelly's, she said, with the bangs parted and "a little poofed out, so I don't look like Alfalfa."

Kelly laughed. "Aleesh loves that show."

Michelle asked about Alicia, and Kelly said, "She's so funny," and started in on how Alicia had gotten in the habit of leaving her Barbie dolls pinched between things—caught in a cupboard door, or stuck between the coffee table and the sofa. Kelly heard herself say this and then set her mind the task of explaining why this was funny, and then lost track of herself talking. When she checked up on herself, there was a silence around her chair.

Michelle seemed to want to ask something more personal, like was Tim making his payments or had she finally started dating again. Kelly could sense when someone was going to try something with her. Michelle was a friend, but it was the same with her guy clients. There was this certain pause before they started hitting on her. They asked about her hobbies, what she liked to do when she was off work, as if they were going to ask her out to do one of those things. Kelly always played against type. If the guy was older or not in great shape, she said she liked rock climbing. If he looked athletic, she said she liked to read or watch TV or garden. This didn't always work, though, and she was forced to bring up her daughter. That usually cooled them down, but not the most dangerous ones. They didn't care if she had a hippopotamus back at her house.

"Your fingers are cold," Michelle said.

"Are they?" Kelly asked.

"Don't you feel cold? I can see goose bumps on your arms."

"They always overdo the air-conditioning in here." Kelly laughed her nervous laugh and kept snipping Michelle's hair.

"God, you've lost weight," Michelle said.

"Have I? I'm not dieting at all. I've just been running around a lot." Kelly glimpsed her arms in the big mirror over her station. She thought her arms had almost nothing extra on them. They were arms, pure arms.

"Girl, watch yourself," Michelle said.

"I do."

"Look, how about coming to the lake with us next weekend?"

"I don't look *that* bad, do I?" Kelly paused in her cutting.

"Kelly? Honestly? Yes."

Kelly cut Michelle's hair, imagining that each strand was a thin blood vessel—a capillary, she remembered from high school biology—coming out of Michelle. It wasn't the first time she had visualized the head of one of her clients running with blood after a haircut. Kelly tried to get rid of such thoughts, but they kept coming back.

"Guys notice that sort of thing," Michelle continued. "They know about it."

"Michelle, you're incredible."

"What? I'm just saying, if you're dieting to get a guy—"

"I'm not dieting to get a guy," Kelly said.

* * *

Mike and Michelle pulled up in their silver Jeep Grand Cherokee, and Kelly, carrying the suitcase, led Alicia down the porch steps to meet them. Kelly finally had agreed to spend the weekend at a big house Michelle and Mike had rented on Lake of the Ozarks. Michelle had more money than Kelly, but Kelly was very pretty. Kelly knew that Michelle was drawn to her because of her appearance. Michelle had a long face with a long nose and hooded eyes; her shoulders were hung slightly to one side, as though her body had taken the shape of a reflection in a fun-house mirror. She was always overweight but, as long as Kelly could remember, had never been without a man.

Mike stepped out of the Jeep and opened the hatchback. Though it was hot out, he wore jeans and cowboy boots. He owned a software company but liked to think of himself as an outdoorsman.

Instead of getting in the Jeep, Alicia followed Kelly to the back, where she was stowing their things.

"There's a man in there," Alicia whispered.

"That's OK," Kelly said. "He won't bite."

Alicia rolled against Kelly's leg.

"Go on," Kelly said. "Get in now."

Kelly wanted Alicia to get in first, to sit between her and the man. That way he'd know how things were. Kelly was very angry with Michelle, for a second, but then it blew over. It didn't matter what the man was like.

She could tell he was tall by the way he was sitting. He was wearing new high-top sneakers and shorts. His legs were covered in golden brown hair. He wore his hair very short on the sides and a little longer on top; it looked as if he got it cut regularly by someone with a nice touch. His shoulders were broad. He wasn't thickly muscled, but his arms looked solid. Everything about him was solid, as if he were made of an entirely different substance from Kelly, though his skin was not good. He was her type. He was her physical type. A thrill went through Kelly. Her eyes teared up. She was mad at Michelle.

The man's name was Greg. His hand was large, solid, rough. He had his own plastering, tuck-pointing, and waterproofing business called Sealmaster. As he told her about it over Alicia's head, Kelly felt an edge to him. Like a saw. He could saw her in half, just by talking to her. He could snap her like a twig. There was something defensive, or aggressive, in his voice. He felt the need to explain to Kelly how a guy with a booming plastering, tuck-pointing, and waterproofing business could afford to take a three-day weekend in the middle of the busy season. His crew could handle things. He mainly bid the jobs and then drove around helping out. He still did everything. He was the boss but he did everything anyway.

"That's nice," Kelly said.

Mike was driving, but he started a discussion with Greg about a crack on the west wall of his brick house that he had to patch every year or two. Mike didn't talk much but he tended to perk up when he was trying to get something. Greg pinned Mike down on the fact that he was using a cement-based compound between the bricks. Greg recommended a mortar with "a little more play to it." He could fix Mike up, if he was interested.

"You know, I might be," Mike said into the rearview mirror.

"Kelly has a brick house," Michelle said significantly, and she smiled.

This was the sort of leading line Michelle used to say back in high school when they double-dated. Michelle usually arranged things then, too. That's how Kelly met the funny alcoholic, Tim. She had divorced him two years earlier for sleeping around on her, for publicly groping her when he was drunk, and, finally (because there had to be a finally), for passing out in an upstairs bedroom just before dinner was served at her mother's Thanksgiving party.

Being humiliated in front of her mother helped her divorce Tim. It was her capitulation to her mother, who herself had capitulated to something, Kelly thought, because she had gotten very fat. Her mother had always told her she was crazy for marrying Tim. "You're so beautiful, you could have any man. And so you pick one who drinks." Her mother taught high school English and was galled by the fact that Kelly was a mediocre student; she rode her mercilessly about her homework until her junior year, when both of them just gave up. Her father had never seemed to care how she did in school. He called her his princess.

As things were ending with Tim, Kelly was having an affair, too, just to protect herself, with one of her clients, the son of a local supermarket mogul. Arnold Westerberg was married and had four perpetually tan, straw-haired kids. She had picked him carefully from the many possibilities for her affair. He was so sweet. But he could also be a whiner—with his huge house in Ladue and the stores he ran and would inherit and his beautiful stay-at-home wife. He had bad dandruff.

Still, she thought she loved Arnold and took him at his word about marrying her once they were both divorced. "How could I be so stupid?" was the formula Kelly settled on for thinking about all this. After Arnold dumped her, she took a cooking class to get out of the house. But when her hollandaise sauces broke or her soufflés refused to rise, she burst into tears. She became subject to sudden terrors, to the old metallic taste of panic. Her throat seemed to swell shut every time she tried to put food in her mouth. She threw out the free groceries Arnold had given her: pounds of frozen shrimp, steaks, cajun chicken breasts, tins of clams and caviar. She fed his Cheerios to the garbage disposal. She had been so stupid—with Tim, with Arnold. Stupid. And dirty. How dirty she had felt when Arnold hugged her for the last time! No more of that. Michelle knew she wanted to stay away from guys—yet here was Greg.

She was very mad at Michelle, but she wasn't going to show it.

Turned sideways in her seat, Michelle took over the conversation, asking questions, making comments, talking about what they could do at the lake (a range of activities requiring expensive, motorized equipment). Kelly became quiet, and Greg did, too, careful to profess as much ignorance as possible about anything unrelated to tuck-pointing, plastering, or waterproofing. In spite of herself, Kelly liked his silence, liked his signs of insecurity. She caught glances of his powerful legs, his strong arms, foaming with beautiful hair. She liked seeing his strength and his insecurity at the same time. If she could have forgotten that Michelle was fixing them up, she might have relaxed.

* * *

The house was as big as Kelly expected, right on the water. The kitchen had an island and overlooked the living room, which had a huge fireplace set in a wall of large stones, a view of the lake through trees, a fifteen-foot ceiling. Michelle and Mike, of course, would have the master bedroom suite. Michelle pointed out the rooms for Kelly and Greg, then gave them a tour through the rest of the house.

The floor they had walked in on was actually the top floor. The level below had a rec room with a pool table, a Ping-Pong table, a big TV, and couches. There was a setup for karaoke, another pair of bedrooms, a sauna. Then they had to go outside and down more stairs (Greg made profuse compliments about the cedar siding), the house crawling down the slope toward the lake, where there were two separate apartments with twin beds and their own kitchens and bathrooms.

Kelly knew that Michelle only showed these apartments so that everyone would appreciate the size of the house, but she said, "This is perfect for Aleesh and me."

Michelle protested that they should all be together upstairs, but Kelly insisted that it was just for sleeping and that she wanted to share a room with Alicia but they should have separate beds. Michelle hadn't thought of this.

"Why not, though?" Greg said. "It's nice down here."

Kelly panicked when Michelle suggested that Greg could stay in the other apartment. Greg seemed ready to answer when Mike reminded Michelle that two other couples were also coming. The Abernathys, who had a young girl, might want the other apartment. The Goffs would no doubt stay upstairs. So it was decided.

When Kelly and Alicia were settling in, Michelle came down with some towels.

"Did you see how considerate he was about you being down here?" Michelle asked. "Kind of makes you wish you were staying upstairs, doesn't it, you ninny."

"Where'd you meet him?"

Michelle said he was a customer at the bank where she worked, plus she'd seen him at Bally's, working out. "Sometimes he even does aerobics."

"A real sweetheart," Kelly said.

"A real sweetheart," Alicia said, sitting on the end of the bed and watching TV.

"It doesn't seem like you know him all that well," Kelly said.

"Kelly? Hello? That's how you make friends. You get to know them."

Kelly was going to reply, but suddenly she ran out of the energy necessary to resist Michelle. She smiled. "That's true," she said. "This place is great."

When Michelle left, Kelly lay on her back on one of the beds. She found herself worrying about making an impression on Greg, even though her body did not want him at all. Something in her mind wanted him—maybe the memory that he was her physical type— but she knew her body would vomit him up. Instead, she would volunteer to make dinner. This had nothing to do with plastering, tuck-pointing, or waterproofing, so it was unlikely that Greg would try to help her. It would set her safely apart.

And when the Goffs and the Abernathys arrived she felt even safer—she could fade to the background, hold still amid all the confusion. She had met them before at Michelle's parties. Geoffrey Goff was a tax lawyer in Clayton, and Clare wrote brochures for a medical supply company. The Abernathys were also a nice couple. Janet was a certified financial planner and Bruce had an online editing business. He wore little rimless glasses the exact shape of his eyes. Janet was petite, pretty, and well-dressed, though she had too many freckles. Kelly felt a little inferior, being just a hairdresser, but she worked at a pretty high-class salon; her clients wore black kimonos over their clothes, and the assistants gave shampoos and neck and scalp massages. Katie Abernathy was ten years old and very thin; she always had a pained expression on her face. Kelly wondered if she would play with Alicia or freeze her out. Alicia had just turned nine, but it was only last Christmas when she finally admitted that Santa Claus was dead. Katie had a knapsack, probably filled with books, small rocks of information that she would hurl at Alicia.

It was late afternoon. Michelle broke out chips and salsa, and she and Kelly handed out drinks. There was talk of getting in a swim before dinner, but everyone was exhausted from the drive and congregated around the kitchen island, sitting on bar stools, praising the house, catching up with one another. All the women except Kelly did aerobics at Bally's, and they talked about instructors. Kelly noticed that Alicia convinced Katie to go down to the rec room with her.

Greg was the newcomer, and he had to field a lot of questions. Everybody seemed interested in him, except Clare. When Michelle introduced them, Clare smiled and said hi but didn't follow up with anything. Greg picked up on this and was especially nice to Clare, quickly turning away questions about himself and instead asking

her about her job. He laughed hard at her jokes. It wasn't a flirta-
tious interest, Kelly thought. In fact, Greg made a point of sitting by
Kelly, of being in her vicinity.

The conversation was lame. Janet Abernathy was bent on talking herself down, describing things she had done or thought of
doing to find out what people thought of her doing or not doing
those things. "Wasn't that stupid?" she would ask. Kelly could tell
that having so many freckles drove Janet crazy. Mike smirked and
concentrated on his Corona, seemingly unaware of the two black
hairs sticking out of his nose. Bruce was eating chips and salsa com-
pulsively, dipping one chip while still chewing another. He wasn't
swallowing fast enough and soon his mouth would overflow. Everyone in the room had a body.

Kelly slipped away to a bathroom. She sat on the toilet lid, thinking she would just catch her breath, but it was uncatchable. Everyone has a body—so what? Not being able to handle this simple
fact made her burst into tears. She got up and washed her trembling hands. What was wrong with her? *What was wrong with her!*
She flushed the toilet, in case anyone was listening for the sound
(though nobody could be listening for the sound) and washed her
hands again. She wasn't going to cry anymore. She wasn't going to
tremble. It was going to stop. She looked at herself in the mirror
with her mouth open, trying to see down her throat, to make sure
it wasn't closing. This suddenly made her yawn deeply. She was going to keep breathing. She examined her face, touched her hair, and
told herself that she was getting control. She sat down again and
closed her eyes and took large breaths, so that her face might return
to normal. After another few minutes, she washed her hands, left
the bathroom, and walked into the living room, where everybody

had moved. The fact that everyone had bodies was more easily accepted, moment by moment—like getting used to a swimming pool that feels cold at first but then turns out to be a good temperature—and then everything was OK.

Clare had enlivened the conversation, talking about staging pictures for her medical catalogs. Once they painted an artificial butt with goo to make it look covered with sores and then photographed it to illustrate a disease some product could cure. Clare made everyone laugh. Kelly liked her, even though she was sort of disgusted by her. Clare had saggy cheeks and a strange body—small on top and wide on the bottom. She was sarcastic in a way that Kelly associated with feminism and political awareness. She caught Clare looking at her, accusingly.

Kelly offered to make dinner. Spaghetti with a red sauce, linguini with clam sauce. A green salad. A chocolate cake with white frosting.

There was nothing in the cupboards. Kelly said she'd go shopping with Alicia. Everybody wanted to come along, but no one followed up. Michelle took Kelly aside and gave her some money. Kelly considered protesting but didn't. She wanted to get out of the house. The images from Clare's gross story were stuck in her mind.

She had her head down, thinking about this, when she almost ran into Greg standing on the front walk.

"Aleesh, honey, you carry the list," she called back to Alicia, who was playing hopscotch on the stone flags. She held out the piece of paper covered with Michelle's loopy handwriting.

"I'll help," Greg said.

"I sure need it," she said, giving up on Alicia and pocketing the list.

There was an awkward moment when they both went straight to the driver's side of the Jeep. But Greg recovered quickly. He even went so far as to sit in the backseat.

The main drag was jammed with cars, simmering in the heat.

"Michelle says you're a hairdresser," Greg said. "I mean, a beauty specialist. What's the word for it?"

"I do hair, basically," Kelly said. Someone cut in front of her and she slammed on the brakes. She did not hit her horn, but Greg powered down his window and yelled out in a fierce voice, "Moron!" His voice boomed: it came from outside the Jeep and through Kelly's closed window, as well as from the backseat. The hot air he let in mixed with the air-conditioned air. Alicia seemed scared for a second, then slunk deeper into her seat, trying to keep from giggling. Kelly didn't know what to say, and it was a while before Greg spoke in a strangled voice. "It figures, Arkansas plates."

Kelly caught a glimpse of him in the mirror, rubbing his face with his hands.

At the grocery store, Greg got control of the cart. It reminded Kelly of how Arnold used to surprise her at Westerberg's and escort her through the aisles. She wanted to grab the cart out of Greg's hands, but he walked on, strong and oblivious.

Alicia had evidently gotten over her shyness around Greg, because now she was trying to get his attention. She did a cartwheel into the cereal aisle, and after Kelly scolded her she walked very slowly, lingering over the products. She fell behind and Kelly had to tell her to keep up. This was an old stunt she used to pull on Tim when she was four or five. They'd all be out at the zoo, or some place, and Alicia would walk as if she were wearing cement shoes until Tim would go back and get her and put her on his shoulders and let her take his sunglasses off and wear them. Greg didn't seem aware that she was flirting with him, but Kelly was angry anyway because Alicia had no right to flirt with him.

"Aleesh!" she called back, very sharply this time.

Alicia paused and then came up to them, obviously stung, and Kelly regretted yelling at her. Alicia had never seemed especially interested in having a stepfather, but Kelly hadn't dated in more than a year. Maybe in the meantime something in Alicia had changed. But something in Kelly had changed, too.

"Help us pick out the noodles," Greg said to Alicia.

Kelly told Alicia to choose two pounds worth. She grabbed two boxes of spiral pasta, and Kelly had to gently talk her into exchanging one for a box of linguini.

"Do you think that'll be enough?" Greg asked. Alicia, familiar with being in the middle of arguments, paused with the boxes over the cart.

"The rule is four dry ounces per person, and there're eight adults," Kelly said, amazed at the effort required to say this with composure. "Aleesh and I will split a portion." Kelly remembered Katie, but that didn't make her change anything.

"That can't be right. Four ounces? Uh-uh. You need at least half a pound a person. I'm a big eater."

"All right," Kelly said. She took the two boxes from Alicia and dropped them in the cart. She grabbed another box before Alicia could do it and proceeded down the aisle without another word. The "uh-uh" really got on her nerves.

Greg hurried after her with the cart. "I don't know why women want to be so skinny," he said. "It doesn't make any sense to me. Eat as much as you want and exercise. That way you don't feel deprived but then you don't really get fat either."

What are you a fucking commercial for? she thought.

"It never made sense to me," he added.

He touched the extra box of pasta. "This is all for you." He smiled.

"Thanks," she said. She was so angry her rib cage was going to burst.

"I'm looking out for you."

"I'm flattered."

Kelly wanted nothing more than to punish Greg and Alicia. She felt justified against them, against everyone. But as they checked out, she made herself smile and said polite things. She couldn't wait to get into the kitchen where no one could follow her.

*   *   *

The red sauce turned out well and Kelly ate some spaghetti. She knew without tasting it that the cake was also good. When she saw other people eating it, she knew she didn't need to have any. She had one beer and it made her drunk. Greg was drinking a lot in a controlled way. He simply drank beer after beer and didn't seem to mind if the shifting of conversations left him sitting alone on a couch. Once he caught Kelly's eye and raised his bottle to her with a stupid boyish smile. Though he was otherwise different from Tim, they both had a capacity for alcohol like a well-developed muscle. Relief washed away the dregs of her anger: she had nothing to do with Greg. She didn't have to divorce him; they were never married, they had never even dated. Michelle had fixed them up, but that was just Michelle.

After dinner, people drifted down to the rec room, to shoot pool and drink more. Greg seemed to have picked up her annoyance over his tagging along to the grocery store, so he didn't press himself on her as he had been. But the fact that he seemed to notice that he had gotten on her nerves made her responsive to him again. As often had happened with Tim, remorse, even tenderness, took the place of her anger. She saw how awkward Greg was with everybody, how he didn't mix well with these people. It wasn't just the type of work he did; there was also a sort of constraint, as if he stuck to talking about his business because if he didn't something else might come up, or he would have to enter into things on another level. Kelly sensed that things were wrenched to the side and amiss in Greg, but she liked him for that. After Alicia went to bed, she asked him if he wanted to be her partner in a game of pool. His face lit up, and she could almost see the teenage boy he used to be, and her heart got warm. Michelle gave Kelly a meaningful look, but Kelly knew that Michelle couldn't understand that all of life wasn't dating or being married. Kelly could just hang out with someone. That's how in control she was.

The first time it was her turn, Greg touched her arm—well, he actually closed his hand around her wrist to point out a shot. She jerked herself free, and that gesture stopped everything in the room, but she quickly said, "Here goes" with a laugh and sank her shot, very neatly. She owed that to long nights out with Tim in the early days. Greg accepted his razzing good-naturedly, and the two of them took on all comers. They were a team. They won every game.

Kelly granted herself a glass of wine—she was on a binge, which surprised her, thrilled her, scared her.

People were getting drunk enough to turn on the karaoke machine, and soon Geoffrey, with his shirt unbuttoned to show his hairy chest, was doing a surprisingly good rendition of "Margaritaville." Even though she was tipsy, there was no way Kelly was going to sing. A long time ago, she had decided that whenever people got creative she would become the spectator. Greg had the same response. United with Kelly during the pool game, he had loosened up; thrown back into the group, he grew shy again. Kelly noticed that he had stopped drinking. She approved of that and stopped her own binge. He nodded his head or beat his hand on his thigh in time to the music, and he applauded each singer—not ironically, like everyone else, but sincerely.

After a while, it became conspicuous that neither Kelly nor Greg had sung a song. Even Janet had done a hilarious "Send in the Clowns." Kelly was surprised when Clare, who was solidly drunk, approached Greg flirtatiously to get him to sing. Kelly wondered if Clare's earlier coolness had concealed a crush, and this made Kelly realize that she herself wanted Greg.

Amazingly, Clare managed to get Greg to stand up. He seemed relieved to be asked by her in particular. They had barely spoken to each other all night, and Kelly thought that maybe Clare with her sharp tongue was the person who made Greg most uneasy. He sorted through the lyric sheets. "Put this on," he said.

It was Johnny Cash's "Ring of Fire." He sang it really well. His awkwardness burned away. His voice had depths and feelings Kelly hadn't imagined. The image of Johnny Cash singing in a prison mixed with the idea of Greg as a soulful outlaw.

"*Love—is a burning thing,*" he crooned.

"I told you so," Michelle whispered in her ear.

Kelly acted as if she were absorbed in watching Greg, which she was, and though this was a poor way to ignore what Michelle had said, Michelle moved on.

"*I fell into a burning ring of fire. I went down, down, down and the flames went higher.*"

Greg didn't point at her, or wink at her, yet she couldn't help but feel that he was singing to her. He didn't do mock lounge-singer moves, as Geoffrey and Bruce and Mike had done. He sang the song as if he'd written it.

Everyone applauded Greg vigorously and he smiled, beaming.

Things wound down. When it came time to say good night, Greg seemed to want to hug Kelly or something. Instead he said, "You're a great pool player."

"You're not so bad yourself."

"All right, see you tomorrow, then."

"All right, Greg." Before she knew it she had said his name. He registered this and looked into her eyes. Kelly turned away and saw the TV. *Change of Heart* was on. A man flipped his card. It said "change of heart." He turned to the woman sitting next to him on the couch and kissed her. The person he had just rejected blew up her bangs with a puff of air. But then she flipped her card—she'd had a change of heart, too. Everyone looked happy.

Greg went upstairs to his room and Kelly headed to her apartment. When she slid open the screen door on the deck, she heard voices. Clare and Janet were sitting on lawn chairs beneath a yellow bug light, looking out over the water. When she came out, they stopped talking.

Clare looked at her and said, "Be careful."

"Excuse me?" Kelly asked.

"Good night, you guys," Janet said, and she slipped off down to her apartment.

"I'm not trying to butt in," Clare said, "but it's about Greg."

Kelly wanted to say "What," but the word stuck in her throat. Instead, she stared at Clare's sagging cheeks, trying to control a surge of contempt.

Clare said, "I know a friend of a friend who I think dated him."

"You think she dated him." She made her voice very flat, one of her mother's techniques for putting people off balance.

"A tall guy named Craig or Greg, from Richmond Heights, with some blue-collar business. Just listen. My friend said that her friend, Kirsten, had a fight with him one night and sent him home, and he left, but he came back and threw a brick through her bedroom window."

"Did she see him?"

"She didn't have to *see* him. He'd pushed her once before. She just got the hell out of town. Got a transfer to Kansas City, I think."

"He doesn't seem like somebody who would do something like that," Kelly said.

Clare sighed. "I know what you mean. But a lot of polite guys are really wound up. They're uptight because they want things to be perfect and when they aren't, they just explode."

"I guess so."

"You could say I don't know for sure," Clare said, "but there's something about him."

She should have thanked Clare for trying to talk her out of Greg; she knew that anything with him would probably turn out horrible and dirty. But she kept thinking about Clare's saggy cheeks, and how smart she was, and she just felt angry, generally, about everything.

"Who knows, maybe it's not him." Clare suddenly laughed and put on one of her sarcastic voices. "Just me speculatin' and ruinin' lives. Well, this has been fun. You're welcome and good night."

After Clare left, Kelly was afraid to go downstairs to the dark apartment. She went back into the rec room and sat down in front of the TV. The credits were rolling on *Change of Heart*, and everybody was standing on the set, bantering. The newly formed couples had one arm behind each other's backs.

* * *

She had a glass of water for breakfast. She didn't even go through the motions of putting something on her plate. Not even a cup of coffee. The others kept snacking until Michelle made sandwiches for lunch. During all this eating, Kelly felt very much alone and took many pointless trips down to the apartment. Alicia wanted to go in the sauna with Katie, but Kelly forbid it and Alicia cried. "Stop crying like a baby," Kelly snapped.

When she came back upstairs, Greg was in a good mood. Instead of sitting hunched over on the couch or in a chair gripping the armrests, he slouched deeply with his feet way out in front of him. Clare praised his singing again, but he immediately turned it into a compliment on Kelly's pool-playing. He went on to make light and friendly conversation with her, but Kelly suddenly needed to apologize to Alicia. She found her in the rec room playing Ping-Pong with Katie. She took Alicia aside, and then, since everyone else was upstairs, she watched Alicia and Katie play until the day's plan took shape: Michelle announced they were all going parasailing.

The fact that she had had nothing to eat all day was making Kelly feel very good, very clean and strong. When she put on her one-piece swimsuit, she wasn't as disgusted as she thought she would be. She wrapped a thin colorful fabric around her legs and tied it at her hip, making a sarong. She put on a gauzy long-sleeve top and her sun hat.

Clare's compliment on Greg's singing made Kelly shake her head. If Clare could flatter him after stabbing him in the back last night, then, really, who was worse: Greg, who maybe had a temper but was honest and passionate, or these two-faced West County–types?

She looked at herself in the mirror and said, "Greg," as if testing how the word matched what she saw. The answer came back immediately: "Stupid. Don't be stupid."

*   *   *

The launch was a beach facing a T-shaped runway of red buoys that went out across the water. You stood on the beach, and workers arrayed the silk sail behind you. Then you stepped into a harness, which prompted feeble bondage jokes from Michelle. They held the sail out behind you and the boat took off and you had to run behind it down the sand and then jump in the air just as you reached the water. Every launch worked, but it looked as if you needed training to do it right. The legs of some people went stiff with terror, but most seemed to enjoy it. The boat went straight out into the lake and then banked sharply to the left, moving around the T. Whenever the boat slowed to turn, the parasailor would sink down, some almost dunking their feet in the water. There were two launch sites, with long lines for both. Michelle kept asking who wanted to go first, but nobody seemed all that eager.

Greg stood apart on the hot sand, in bare feet, wearing swim shorts and a plain, worn, white T-shirt. Kelly let the wind blow her hair across her eyes; through her hair, she looked at his legs. Alicia came over and took her hand. She quietly begged Kelly not to have to fly around. Kelly was happy to reassure her. She wanted to impress her daughter with what she was about to do.

The rest of the gang was lost in excitable chatter. Greg asked Kelly if she wanted to sign up. They walked over to the table and paid twenty dollars and signed the list and the release form. She signed her name, then Greg did. Eventually everyone signed up except Clare. "Someone has to call your next of kin," she said.

"I wish it went on longer," Kelly said, watching someone fly high above the top of the T, legs hanging loose.

Greg said, "Yeah." He shifted his feet, putting himself a half step closer to her.

"Are you sure you'll fly?" Kelly asked in a light tone, despite feeling an unpleasant charge from his closeness. "Guys like you eat bricks for breakfast, don't you?"

Greg barked a laugh. The mention of bricks didn't give him pause at all. "No, I'm totally hollow," he said. "Here, knock on top of my head." He offered her the top of his head.

"You're nervous," Kelly said.

"I am," he admitted. He made an O with his mouth and rapped on his skull with his knuckles, making a hollow coconut sound. He laughed and Kelly laughed.

The boat was finishing a run. It streamed straight for them, trailing the parasailor. Suddenly, the boat cut its engine and banked, sending a wave of water onto the beach. The parasailor lost momentum, dropped from the sky, and splashed into the lake.

* * *

When it was time for Kelly to slip off her sandals and her straw hat and her gauzy blouse and her wrapskirt, she felt Greg's eyes on her. Hard shell, but hollow. Kelly understood him. She knew she did. She expected he would be impressed by her body, though for a second her own kneecaps seemed grotesquely large to her. There was a pleasant lightness in her head and butterflies in her stomach that she hadn't felt for years. Her feet hardly sank in the sand.

Walking slowly toward the harness was the way she wanted everyone to see her, and for the first time that weekend she felt as though she were taking her proper place in the group. As the workers clicked the straps on her she felt even better, confirmed, secure. Seeing the boat and the runway before her, with no one else in sight, gave her a stab of fear, but it passed. She was meant to be alone in just this way.

All at once the boat roared and she ran after it down the beach, her sail bouncing behind like a tin can on a wedding limo. When she approached the water, she jumped into the air as if she were leaping off a diving board. She pulled her legs up into her stomach, realized she had risen quickly and lightly, then let her legs dangle. She ascended rapidly, in quick, accelerating jerks, like a kite on a very windy day. She remembered riding a roller coaster with Tim and how her stomach would clench as they careened down a big hill, and she expected those painful sensations now, but it was as if her stomach had melted away, as if she no longer had such a thing in her body. She had had nothing, not a thing, to eat since the glass of wine that marked the peak and the end of last night's binge. The water and the landscape dropped away just as it had when she took that thirty-seater airplane to Springfield. The view was like being in that plane right after takeoff, except she was surrounded by nothing, as if she had shed her body to become pure soul in the wind.

Her legs blew to one side and swayed further when the stiff wind gusted. Even when the boat turned, she hardly dipped toward the water as the others had. She was different, lighter, above them all. The boat, the silk snapping and billowing over her head, the bar she held onto—these were all incidental. They tracked her and framed her, but she was actually flying by herself. The moment seemed to trump every stupid thing she had ever done—that's how good it felt. The boat turned again, then streaked parallel to the shore. The wind was coming from this direction and lifted her even higher. The updraft was exhilarating, not painful. She could see beyond the clumps of trees like broccoli, to the main drag and all the cars and low flat buildings and billboards. There were pockets of warmer and cooler air as she soared over the lake. She remembered the mix of hot and cool air when Greg had yelled out the Jeep window. Clare was probably right about him.

But up here, she could face that. She was untouchable, unafraid of him. She knew him better and could handle him better than any Clare Goff or Kirsten Whoever could. That was what was really tempting about him, beyond his body and his beautiful hair: maybe he had a certain problem, maybe he might be so angry with himself, or so fearful about something, that he might do things that he himself hated to do—but she felt she knew him.

This was a stupid temptation. It was an insane indulgence. But she couldn't help being drawn to where the feelings were. "Feel something," she said aloud, as if she were reasoning with herself.

The boat banked again and headed down the runway on which she had started. She was being dragged back toward the shore, heading right for Alicia, who was waving wildly, and Janet and Clare and Bruce and Katie and Geoffrey and Michelle and Mike and Greg. Just then the boat banked sharply and the tension on her harness stopped and she felt herself about to fall.

After descending a bit, she felt a strong gust of wind lift her again. She hovered for an instant, then another gust struck under her left arm and raised her, pushing her away from the landing area toward the other launch. She laughed. Her whole body tingled in the wind that buffeted her and lifted her and made her hover. This force wasn't the regular pull of the boat but the element she had been riding the entire time—the wind, the raw and irregular wind. She *knew* the wind! She was overjoyed to see astonishment and panic in the faces of her friends, mixed with—was it jealousy or disgust? She was too light to fall! Fifty feet above them and sliding to the side. What if she weighed only fifty pounds? Or forty? What if she would never land?

Greg came splashing into the water, angling for where she was headed. The next gust couldn't lift her as much, and he adjusted his running so that it became clear they were converging on a jagged path. As the wind faltered, she began to shake with what might have been crying if she didn't suddenly feel so absolutely like the dried husk of an insect—something her spirit had left behind. She drifted down, swaying sliding hovering over Greg. His face was determined, his eyes on her feet. His powerful legs thrashed the water as he tracked her. There were no words of comfort, no cries for help. Down. Down. His hand closed painfully on her ankle. She kicked once without loosening his grip, instantly lost all buoyancy, and found herself landed in his arms.

Admit

The juggler in front of Brine Sporting Goods balanced a Star Market shopping cart on his chin. I felt pressure on my own face and hoped this was the beginning of a new joke. *Isn't juggling weird?* I imagined asking on stage at Nick's Comedy Stop. I couldn't complete the joke, and I still felt pressure on my face. About twenty people stood around watching the juggler. The whole scene was frozen and semi-horrible. It seemed like a good idea to get away from this juggler.

I continued down Brattle Street, my law textbooks pulling my backpack hard against my sweating shoulders. After I'd staggered out of Contracts, my notebook filled with gags and stray references to case law, I just kept walking, gravitating toward the hubbub of Harvard Square. It was early May. After forty-five days of rain, the sky was a perfect blue, the breeze warm. I was getting angry because I wasn't enjoying it. I entered a red-brick crosswalk with a mob of pedestrians, made a beeline for the postcard racks at Out of Town News. I would send my psychotically ambitious friends in Chicago and NYC messages like "You are in material breach!" or "Guilty as charged!" or "Help me," all signed "Tortfeasor." Something to put them off balance.

Hoping to erase the residue of vicarious shopping-cart pressure, I rubbed my chin vigorously. I hadn't heard the applause that always accompanied the dismount of the cart. Maybe the handle still nestled against the juggler's lower lip like an elaborate orthodontic appliance. I plucked a postcard off the rack—a picture of Out of Town News itself. I was thinking of penning myself into the image when a shadow passed over the card. It could have been an airplane, because no matter how high they fly their shadows can touch the ground, or maybe it was a freak interposition of the body of a flying bird. It occurred to me that for any given bird, this interposition became exponentially more likely the closer the bird. This thought made the pressure on my chin spread to my entire head, encasing my brain like a helmet. A wild skateboarding punk rocker disturbed a covey of pigeons, which rose leadenly into the air, swooped in ragged formation not far from my face, then settled near me to tear into a discarded bag of popcorn. I had the uncanny feeling that a basket of metal was plummeting toward my head, and the panic that struck me was strong and pure. Still clutching the postcard, I bolted for the nearby T entrance and got underground immediately, where I called Lisa.

"Lisa, do me a huge favor and pick me up from the Porter Square T station in like ten minutes, OK?"

"David, I'm trying to work here."

"You need a break. You're worn out."

"What?"

"Could you just please?" The relative calm of my voice contrasted in a fascinating way with the spastic galloping of my heart. I could have wrung a quarter cup of sweat out of my T-shirt.

She hung up without another word.

Isn't juggling stupid? I thought, hearing it in my stage voice. *I mean, don't people have enough problems as it is? "So if I can just get three flaming knives going, maybe I can swing a hula hoop on my ankle." Cut it out, you idiots! Give us all a break!*

I wrote this down in my pocket humorist's notebook and tried to evaluate my joke. It seemed angry. It didn't make me smile at all. If I'd heard it myself, I wouldn't have laughed.

* * *

Though Lisa was miffed, she cared about me for some reason, and she was waiting when I surfaced. As we rode to our apartment on Somerville Ave., I tried to explain what had happened. Between shifting gears, she pulled at her long, wavy hair. "David," she said, "if you don't start seeing someone, I'm going to be very pissed off."

"I know how this looks, but I'm totally sane. I'm freaking out *because* I'm totally sane."

Lisa sighed heavily. We'd had a million conversations in which I'd tried to explain how hard it was for me to figure out what to do with my life. I was a 1L at Harvard, and I loved the prestige of that, but I'd recently become convinced that I was so funny I should be a professional humorist instead of a lawyer.

"I thought I could drop out today," I added, experimentally.

"Then leave. Give it a try."

"But then, when I was walking around the Square, I just didn't feel funny."

"David."

"It was like I was antifunny. Every thought I had was unfunny." I couldn't bring myself to tell her my new juggler joke.

"I keep telling you you're pressing too hard; just relax about it."

She hit the flat of one palm against the steering wheel for emphasis.

"Neither of us is relaxed," I said unhelpfully.

She drove with her hands at eleven and one. With her shoulders hunched, she looked like a praying mantis. "Well, what do you expect? Jesus, David, it's like living with Eeyore. 'We're doomed, we'll never make it.'"

I laughed uproariously, way out of proportion to the joke, but I loved when she made fun of me. It made me think I belonged with her after all.

"Actually," I said, "I see myself as more of a Tantalus figure."

My laughter made her relent toward me, so I heard expectant listening in her silence. But I froze over the explanation, which I had just formulated the other day. Ever since I had begun thinking seriously about a career in comedy, I had experienced a Tantalus-like relationship to my sense of humor: when I dipped to drink, it receded.

"Whatever," she said. Then she added, as if the war were back on: "God, David, you need a shower."

"I know," I said.

Lately I'd noticed that my nervous perspiration had a certain extra pungency compared to my physical exertion perspiration. It was a development I was watching out of the corner of my eye.

* * *

While I made us a spaghetti dinner with too much garlic, I thought about whether in fact I needed professional help. I had seen a counselor at the law school for a while. Ron was "intrigued" that I was considering dropping out. Most of his clients, he said, were anxious about "making it" in the big-shot law world; he didn't often talk to students who wanted to walk away. I told him my concern: it would be depressing to flounder around as a stand-up comic for years, working crap jobs, when I could be making more than 100K a year at a NYC firm. He told me that Kurt Vonnegut lived in a constant state of depression while he produced his great comedic fictions. This had actually heartened me a bit: OK, fine, I thought, I'll live in a constant state of depression, but at least I'll be pursuing what I really want. "Whatever you do," Ron added meaningfully, "you need to be in a structured environment."

That had caught me off guard, but now I wondered if an underground bunker would qualify as a structured environment. Maybe there was a joke there. I turned it over in my mind.

While I was emptying a can of tomato paste to thicken the spaghetti sauce, Lisa slapped her enormous textbook shut, stood up from the futon couch, and stretched. From the stove, I spied her smooth belly, and a bolt of yearning entered my mind. She brought her fists down to her sides, bounced on her toes, and made a tension-releasing throaty roar. It seemed that I wanted her physically.

After dinner, I took a shower and joined her on the couch. I had some Property to read, and she studied how cells in the body were actually computers with DNA software. She put her head on my lap, and I balanced my ten-pound textbook on the wooden arm of the futon couch. While she read, she rested her book on her belly and picked at her toes. I ran my eyes over paragraph after paragraph of *Pennsylvania Coal v. Mahon* without grasping a single word. She playfully rolled her head against my groin.

"Anyone home?" she asked.

"Sure," I answered, without a trace of ease.

We dumped our books and began groping. She slipped me out of my shorts before I was ready. I tongued the three dark hairs in her right areola while wondering why I was treating these hairs as if they were three separate beings who lived on the surface of her body. She took off her own shorts and appeared to want me to enter her. I wasn't ready, so I moved down for cunnilingus. I was industrious and sort of rhythmic. I thought something might be building, but when I moved my tongue to a part of her labia I'd temporarily neglected, it was slick but cool to the touch.

After another ten minutes in which I felt as if I were leaking through a sieve, we managed to copulate. In all our time together, I never once gave her an orgasm, despite logging hundreds of hours inside her.

But our postcoital cuddling could be intense. Maybe because of my earlier panic attack, it was one of those nights when we clung to each other. We repaired to the bedroom. The alley light was shining through the blinds. When we first moved in, I thought this was cool, your basic bohemian ambience, but now the light struck me as a lidless eye, the emblem of my sleep-impoverished nights. Lisa lay with her head on my chest, giving my torso one-armed hugs. I squeezed her, too. But I started to feel strange and pathetic, so I got up and gave her a back scratch, which she liked more than sex, hands down.

"I really like licking you," I said while scratching, hoping to start one of those frank conversations about sex that break through some silly but potent inhibition and change a couple's lovemaking forever. Of course, I also heard how that sounded and cracked up laughing.

Lisa laughed, too, her cheek turned against the pillow. "You *are* funny, David," she said. "Weird funny."

"Do you want to hear my new joke?" Oddly enough, I had thought of it during our lame sex act.

"Yeah."

"It's just sort of a *New Yorker* cartoon. A dictator with a thoughtful look on his face is talking to an aide. The dictator says, *'It's not the assassination attempt itself, but the* tone *in which it was carried out.'*"

Lisa laughed a bit. "David, you should try. Twenty years from now you'll be kicking yourself if you don't."

A bus hurtled down Somerville Ave. at about seventy miles per hour, shaking our wooden building.

"I should go," I said, and I stopped scratching Lisa's skin.

"Law school is making you insane," she said, turning over to face me.

"I'll go," I said.

"Sure," she said.

"I'll get the leave of absence."

She sighed. "Do it with a leave then. You've got to do what you want."

Lisa still said idiotic things like "follow your bliss" and "you can do whatever you set your mind to." When we met as seniors at Northwestern, she'd really gotten off on the fact that I was admitted to Harvard Law and she was headed for a monster biomedical engineering program put together by MIT and Harvard Med School. It seemed as if we *could* do whatever we wanted together—even though she was Jewish and I wasn't and her parents didn't like that. But those lines always made me uncomfortable, because they implied success was simply a matter of deciding and following through. That this wasn't true frightened me; that it *was* true frightened me as well.

"Yeah, but it means living in LA for a while," I said.

"Just for a year, you said."

"Yeah, but if I make it—I mean, the whole point is if I make it—"

"You should go," she said.

I realized this sentence would work equally well as the climax to a year of pep talks or as the shattering end to a long fight. Either way, something was breaking up.

* * *

I lived in North Hollywood, an abject concrete and stucco shithole, a very good argument against the human race. I would temp for a while to get a wad of cash (once at an entertainment law firm, once in the Paramount Story Department, once at a place that did nothing but buy and sell golf courses), then work nonstop on my stand-up routine and spec scripts.

A cornerstone of my stand-up act was talking about the toll drinking was taking on my life. I didn't actually drink very much at all, except on certain occasions when I drank a ton, but I was convinced that alcoholism was funny. I'd say, "You know you've had too much to drink when the first thing you hear the next day is, 'Look, he's awake!'" I'd say, "My idea of multitasking is drinking and driving." I claimed that grocery store parking lots were my favorite place to imbibe. I also did this character, the nonchalant fireman, whose tag lines were "a little fire never hurt anyone" and "it'll burn itself out."

Which is to say, I didn't go completely unlaughed at, yet neither did people always laugh or laugh with the abandon that would make them remember my name, and also sometimes things fell awkwardly silent at significant moments in my routine. Still, the club owners I met and the audience members I stood in front of and the waitresses who smirked at me when they saw me at the pay phone after my set, dialing Lisa to give her the lowdown—all these people took it for granted that I was a comedian.

After spending months cruising the open mikes and occasionally landing a slot at a rinky-dink club, it was time to make a video of my act so I could send the tape to the people who put together the showcases for the producers and scouts and casting types. This was the whole reason to be doing stand-up in LA as opposed to Boston. There was a key moment in my act, right near the end, where I segued from alcohol to my final jokes. I'd say, "As soon as I get my drinking where I want it, I'm moving on. Gonna write a book. I'm going to call it *Thighs in My Pants: The Autobiography of a Legless Man.*"

This was an extremely high-risk joke. It was a crowning, non sequitur absurdity and as such the routine had to be going great to set it up. Plus it depended on the subtle way I presented my two-legged body to the audience. It was a line I'd ad-libbed during a really good gig and somehow it had brought down the house. But it seemed to grow less and less funny the more I used it. Should I change this when I did my tape? I entered this state of mind where this line was the key to my entire routine and, therefore, to my entire life.

The problem was, the taping was very expensive, especially if I wanted the sound quality that everyone told me was crucial, so a "do over" was impossible. This tape would be my calling card, my whole damn self, and, lo and behold, the Tantalus effect kicked in big time. I tried a bazillion substitute jokes without success, and the night of my taping I just went with the joke that had worked a few times, as opposed to the new stuff that never really worked.

Of course, when I got to that legless line during the taping, I froze the house: the silence was so perfect that any watcher would think the audio channel had been cut during recording.

On the heels of this catastrophe, spring registration for next fall at the law school rolled around. I decided to register, to be on the safe side, and also pay Lisa a visit. When I had told her about my video fiasco, I unexpectedly began crying into the phone. Lisa seemed to take this in stride, but near the end of the conversation, after her obligatory pep talk, she said simply, "Something is happening to you, David."

I didn't know what to say to that, but when I hung up the phone, I was sure that something was happening to *us*, and that I'd better get back to Cambridge to make sure it didn't keep happening.

* * *

Registration was on the top floor of Austin Hall, in the big courtroom where they held the moot court finals. It's a high-ceilinged room with big wooden buttresses, like a church. When I walked in after being away from Harvard for nine months, I was shocked by how loud and confident everyone sounded. It was like a cocktail party turned up a thousand decibels: people were declaiming in tight groups of two or three, some with their feet set wide apart, some gesticulating as if they were conducting symphony orchestras, some laughing with exaggerated enthusiasm, bending over and clapping their hands, like I've seen Tom Cruise do. The line to register was short; people were mostly socializing. I went in there

wearing a T-shirt and jeans and, among these smartly dressed mil-
lionaires-in-training, I felt like a stray teenager from a youth-group
car wash. This was 2L registration only. All of my pals from the first
year—and there weren't a lot to begin with—had already registered
as 3Ls. The prospect of returning to law school and knowing very
few people in my classes made me feel extremely lonely.

After registration, I cut through the walled and gated Yard toward Lisa's. She was living with this woman, Madhu, in a condo on
Ellery Street. Madhu's dad had bought it for her while she would be
attending MIT's Sloan School for an MBA. At first I had really liked
the idea of Lisa living with Madhu, but the place had turned into
Boys Central. As I stepped out of the elevator and heard deep male
laughter behind the door to 3A, I got a bit antsy.

Inside, clustered around the kitchen island, were Lisa and three
Sloan schoolers: the aforementioned Madhu, a strikingly beautiful
woman whose parents were from Delhi; Madhu's boyfriend, Mark,
a blond, squeaky clean, marathon-running Swarthmore boy who
wanted to spend his life "making deals"; and William Weintraub, a
really handsome, broad-shouldered, curly-haired Jewish dude who,
I instantly concluded, was well on his way toward replacing me in
the affections of Lisa.

Lisa kissed the air near my cheek and gave one of my hands a
companionable squeeze. There were handshakes all around as the
circle broadened to accept me. Madhu returned the group to B-
school gossip, and, as I listened to who spent summers where and
what the average starting salaries were with the investment banks
and how the dot-com thing was going to be huge (Weintraub was
about ready to punt on B-school altogether and head west to start-
up land), I more or less shut down.

Which meant that I couldn't find my entry points into the conversation. Lisa shot me many glances that said I was childish, self-absorbed, a huge snob.

Meanwhile, Weintraub took the floor. He went on and on about "driving the market," "leveraging core competencies," and building "first mover" advantages that would make "VCs" slobber all over his broad shoulders.

At one point, Mark, who was actually a nice guy, asked me how things were at "HLS."

"I don't know," I said. "There's something overdone about a lot of the personalities there—a lot of bombastic people who are sort of friendly to you, but you can tell they've got number one in mind 24/7."

That outburst was a real conversation killer. Lisa explained, "David is a writer—he's always really critical of stuff."

"I'm not a writer," I said, though I lacked the courage to tell the group that I would like to be a "humorist." That might have gotten a laugh, because, to them, I was obviously a dour, socially awkward, unfunny person.

Still, Lisa and I went to Casa Mexico that night, just the two of us, as if we were a happy couple. The skull of a cow on the wall above our table set the tone. I scarfed basket after basket of brittle tortilla chips and drank water by the pitcher. The conversation ranged from the menu to the decor to the weather to the decor to, eventually, whether we liked our food. Getting desperate, I asked Lisa how much she would give me if I walked out wearing one of the sombreros hanging on the wall. She sighed, and I was so afraid of having nothing substantial to talk to her about that I began shredding Weintraub. I quoted him in a totally unfair caricature of his voice and told Lisa flat out: "Suckering for the jargon of your field is a sign of insanity."

I thought she was going to respond with one of her "you're afraid of success" speeches, but instead she asked me how registration went. I said, "Swimmingly. I'm back in the saddle again."

Lisa asked for the check, which I'd never seen her do before. We split it.

Back at her condo, I waited until she was almost done getting ready for bed, and then I started getting ready, too, looking for the stop and go lights. She didn't say anything when I got into bed with her, and it wasn't until we'd been kissing and holding for a while that she said, "Stop."

I did.

"I don't know what I am to you," she said, and she seemed very close to crying, but she didn't cry.

"I think you're Lisa."

"You just need somebody or some*thing*." Her own comment plunged her into thought. "I'm not sure I want to be on the receiving end of you anymore. I feel like I'm just . . ."

I did what I usually did during a relationship crisis: got silent and thought about what had been said to me and found, or invented, the way it was supposed to hurt me and then indulged in that pain, until my silence made the other person say something different, feel sorry for me, take a different tack.

But Lisa didn't say anything more. This unnerved me, so I began yammering. I said I didn't blame her for being uncomfortable around me because I felt very uncomfortable around myself. I told her about how lonely I'd felt during registration, how after moving so quickly through the air from North Hollywood to Harvard, my identity was experiencing jet lag. She listened silently; it was like bombing in front of an audience. I almost said I was "lost," but I knew how pathetic that would sound. Still, just the word in my head was hard to take. Unfortunately, I started sort of weeping.

Lisa responded with shoulder pats. "It'll be all right," she said.

"Possibly," I said.

After a time, she sighed and rolled over, her face to the wall. I felt as stiff as the plank on a pirate ship and noticed I was lying on her bed at a slight angle with my arms at my sides. Before she could fall asleep, I dropped out of bed with my pillow and got down on the plush cream carpet. I lay there with my eyes open for about three hours. Finally, I slipped out of the room and into the kitchen, where I used her cordless to call the airline and whisper my way to a flight change for a reasonable fee. By 7:00 AM, on a dark, cool, thickly cloudy morning, I was going underground to the T at Central Square, on my way to Logan.

The rest happened by phone. Lisa said she still cared about me, but she was "ambivalent" about our relationship. In the middle of June, she would leave for a month in Europe, Hong Kong, and Japan, on one of those world tours that seem to be the inalienable right of people who are headed for high-powered careers. She didn't mind telling me she was going to rendezvous with Weintraub in Hong Kong, where he'd be traveling with a group of Sloan schoolers on a "meccas of capitalism" educational junket. I was trying to say goodbye and bon voyage when the next thing I knew we were broken up finally and totally and for good.

Meanwhile, I kept trying in LA, and, as my scheduled return to law school neared, I had many psychotic moments of truth in which I decided and undecided my future on almost a minute-to-minute basis. When a spec script was returned without sparking interest or on nights when I did stand-up for a crowd of four people and got paid ten dollars and a bacon cheeseburger, I thanked my lucky stars I had HLS in my back pocket, but when I thought of sitting high in the tiers of a classroom like Langdell North Middle, trying to get my mind around Corporations while my peers tapped notes into their laptops, I felt a death vibe. The legal world seemed cold and scary and depressing, and even though I was at a big-shot school, I had no sense that I could do the work out in the world where it mattered.

I returned to Cambridge in a quasi-daze. I was living in Dane Hall, on the first floor, mainly with 1Ls and international students. I had gone for the dorm thing in order to meet people and also because returning a housing form and looking for my own apartment required vastly different amounts of effort. I tried to harness myself to Corporations, Con. Law, Evidence and Poverty. I was now toying with public interest stuff to avoid becoming a corporate fascist. The problem was that I wasn't sleeping normally, and as the work picked up and I doubted whether I could do it, I began to defecate four, five, six times a day. My nervous bowels were constantly emptying themselves, maybe thinking in their blind way that I was about to enter some great gladiatorial combat, for which a light stomach would be an advantage.

My mother had sensed I was going off the rails again and was calling all the time, to keep me on the lawyer track.

"You don't realize how lucky you are," she said one night on the phone from Berea, Ohio, the Cleveland suburb where I'd lived my whole life before going to Northwestern. "You don't realize that you've already made it."

Dad, on the extension, was silent.

I said, "Yeah, I know."

"It took you a while to get used to college, too," Mom said. "Just think things through."

"It's hard to know exactly what to think."

"I think you know," Mom said. "I think you already know what to do."

I avoided dairy products and spicy foods. Finally, I went to see a doctor in the Holyoke Center. To prepare for my visit, I had picked up a little cardboard container exactly like the pints for Ben and Jerry's ice cream. I took it home, pooped into it, and dutifully carried it in my backpack across Harvard Yard to my appointment. Strangely enough, that walk is one of my most indelible memories of HLS.

Numerous tests run on my stool sample showed absolutely nothing wrong with me, so I went on messing with my diet and defecating so often I was worse than raw. My only jolt of confidence during this entire period was when I hit on using A&D ointment, the stuff for preventing diaper rash, to keep my anus lubed and somewhat soothed.

This whole time I kept making and re-making the decision whether to stay or drop out. The HLS catalog published a table showing how much tuition you'd get back if you withdrew by a certain date, so an extra sense of crisis loomed near those deadlines. My parents weren't able to help with my expenses, and I was taking out huge loans, which seemed to create an extended indentured servitude between me and the law, especially if I was intent on refusing to become a corporate tool.

Lisa and I had stayed friends. I needed her friendship badly. With my insomnia and hyperactive bowels, plus a flaky rash burgeoning on my neck under each ear, and my alienation from my law school peers, I needed a familiar person to talk to. She encouraged me to keep doing stand-up, so even though my semester, academically, was like a car accident in slow motion, I did a few open mikes. I turned the stool sample into part of my act, and some people laughed at me.

As exams approached, I tried very hard to put some outlines together. Physically, the months of not sleeping and excessive defecation were taking their toll, yet I felt preternaturally clearheaded, as if my thought muscles had become incredibly buff from excessive worrying. Standing outside the huge doors of Langdell North Middle before the Corporations final, chatting with my acquaintances in that course, I launched into a speech critical of the venerable pursuit of corporate law, asserting "you're not a real player" when all you do is word someone else's agreements or defend someone else's rapacious behavior in court. I went so far as to claim that being a corporate lawyer amounted to being a kind of restroom attendant who "shook off" the penises of executives after they urinated. Consequently, this would be my last law school exam ever. People smiled awkwardly at these pronouncements. Then we went in and printed our ID numbers on the covers of the blue books and wrote the godforsaken exam.

Afterward, something strange happened when I was standing in Harkness Commons, talking to my peers about the test. Someone was asking how we'd all responded to one of the questions. I wanted to say that it was stupid to talk about an exam after the exam has been taken, but instead of saying this, I noticed a taste of tin in my mouth, which precipitated a strange hiccup in my train of thought. I swear I didn't think I would make it to the other side of that hiccup. In the meantime, the world turned hyperreal and horrid and overlit and clear, and I felt pressure in my ears. Luckily for me, someone in the group suggested we all go to dinner. I was so relieved to be included that the hiccup passed.

Still, back in Berea for break, I felt as if I were on furlough from a war zone. One night, during a beautiful, big-flaked snowstorm, I had a long phone conversation with Lisa in which she told me that Weintraub had decamped to Silicon Valley without finishing his MBA and things were over between them. This show of vulnerability on her part made me respond with a litany of my own problems, from my intestinal issues to my disturbing moment after the Corporations exam. Our mutual miseries worked Lisa into a sort of passion. She unleashed a diatribe about how "ambition makes people into monsters" and nobody does what they really love and nobody is capable of loving anyone at all. I couldn't tell if she was referring to Weintraub, or me, or herself—or all three of us. We ended up talking for hours, and I felt closer to her than I ever had before. I almost hinted about getting back together, but I didn't want to spoil the conversation. Instead, I told her I was dropping out for good and choosing comedy once and for all because I really liked it and didn't care if I failed at it. I believed that if I "went for it" and "followed my bliss," everything would turn out. "I don't need to be a big shot anymore," I told Lisa, and she said, sincerely, "Good for you, David." As soon as I got off the phone, I typed up a letter of withdrawal from Harvard Law School.

I wouldn't say I was manic the next morning, but I was enjoying the moment and what I was doing with it. I picked up the sealed letter and went outside. It was a sunny day, warmish for January. The previous night's snow had covered everything in white, but the asphalt street was dark with melt. It glinted and shimmered in the sun. I had shoveled my parents' driveway that morning and it was clear and wet. I went down the driveway to the mailbox right before noon, because the mailman always came before one o'clock and I didn't want too much of a chance to change my mind. I opened the door of the mailbox and put in my withdrawal letter, lifted the red flag, and walked back to my parents' split-level house.

But by the time I returned to the front door, I knew nothing had changed. I was still me—fearful of everything, as unfunny as ever—but now I had peeled the little "Harvard" sticker off my forehead. Yet I also knew that to go back to the mailbox and remove the letter meant that I would never escape the decision. If I could show no will, I was doomed.

I stood on the porch, right in front of the door, thinking about this. At a certain point, I turned and faced the street, as if I were going back to the mailbox, but I didn't move. After another ten minutes, the mailman appeared, going from box to box in his truck. When he finished with our neighbor's and accelerated toward ours, I headed down the driveway, maybe to stop him, but when I reached the street, he was done. He waved to me, and I waved back at him. When he drove away, the red flag was down. Within a week, I was defecating like a normal human being.

* * *

I flew back to Boston and found myself an apartment. With some student loan money left over and a tuition rebate coming, I decided not to get a job. I was just going to buckle down and be extremely funny all the time.

I spent a lot of time walking the streets, looking for hilarious events to record in my humorist's notebook, and scrutinizing sitcoms to hone my sense of rhythm. I practiced new stand-up material into a tape recorder and had six spec scripts going simultaneously. I didn't want to think too much about whether this material was any good. The point was to fend off the Tantalus effect, to produce, produce, produce. As long as my batting average was greater than zero, sheer volume would carry me toward laughter.

Months went by while I performed, sent out, and queried without a breakthrough. Soon the grace period on my loans would expire and I would have to get a job. The day I realized this, I also acknowledged the new stuff I'd worked into my routine wasn't totally effective. I thought maybe this was because the new material was subtly clashing with the old and throwing everything off. I decided to force the issue. One Sunday night, I took only recent material to an open mike at The Comedy Connection.

It was a decent crowd, mainly tourists, about forty people. Waiting my turn, I paced around by the bar, nursing a Sprite. I saw through every joke the other comedians told. When I finally took the stage, I was shaking my head, subtly signaling to the audience that my new stuff was all about what a useless piece of shit I was. "I'm a *horrible* lover," I said, taking the mike off the stand. The lights seemed too bright. I couldn't really see people. "Really awful. Last night I'm having sex with my girlfriend, and the phone rings. She answers it." This got a few start-up laughs. I moved my hips and torso as if I were a woman on top of a guy and acted out a one-sided conversation, holding my free hand to my face like a phone: "'Hey Jimmy, how *are* you?' . . . 'Yeah?' . . . 'Me? Oh, not much.'" A decent laugh. "Meanwhile, I'm like—" And I leaned back as if I were on the bottom and did a palsied upward humping motion with a twisted look on my face. More people laughed. I straightened up and shook my head. "People say I should get out of the relationship, go where I'll get some respect from a woman, but I can't afford the drinks at strip clubs." A passable laugh.

I don't want to quote much more from that gig. I will admit, though, that I talked about how I was a law school dropout, pretty much an unmitigated failure at life. The laughs dwindled as I went on beating myself up, turning comedy into something else. At one point, I ad-libbed, "I've got shit for brains, have you noticed that?" and the audience just dead-eyed me.

Then a waitress dumped half a hutch of glassware on the floor.

I said, "Ah, what a relief." But nobody got it. Heads turned to view the mess.

A heckler yelled, "Hey, at least you're not the only one getting fired tonight."

When I reached for a comeback, I heard with startling clarity the sound of kicked broken glass tinkling across the floor. I put my hand across my brow to see through the glare and said simply, "What the fuck are you saying?"

If the heckler had persisted, I might have fought back in a better way, and then what happened might not have happened, but the room went silent. I had the bizarre sense that a corresponding silence in me was speaking with the audience's silence and, even weirder, that this conversation was going on behind my back.

I pondered this betrayal for an unknown number of seconds, unable to reconnect with myself as a comedian near the end of a routine. When I saw this pause could last forever, something went very wrong with how the world felt, with how it was lit.

The next thing I knew, I had stepped off the front of the stage and was heading down a tunnel of perception to the door. I passed an agent I recognized just as I was trying to remember where my coat was. He said, "Don't quit your day job." It seemed illegal that someone could use such a cliché in real life and mean it so sincerely—and direct it at me. I shoved this man. I shoved past him on my way out of the club. It was physical violence. He called out, "Sayonara, asshole! You'll never gig in this town again!"

I went out the door and into a drizzly Quincy Market. What had started happening to me on stage was still happening. It was exciting and interesting and frightening. The sense of mundane horror was very startling, far more intense than the moment after the Corporations exam. It seemed that a very uncanny lens had fallen across my vision. I became hyperconscious of each streetlight and store sign pushing physically against total blackness.

I was wearing an idiotic sport coat and decided not to go back for my jacket. I got on my bike and pedaled down State Street, around the curve of Government Center, and then down the hill of Cambridge Street. The hissing of many tires against wet pavement filled the air. As usual, I was almost killed getting through the intersection at Charles Street, but as I pumped over the Longfellow Bridge, and the Red Line T rattled by like the literal projection of a train of thought I was having and which was getting ahead of me, I felt no relief, only a deepening sense of unreality and sickness.

I got home and took a shower. It was about 10:00 PM. I lived in a studio apartment on Highland Ave. in Somerville with an excellent view of planes headed for landings at Logan. I watched the blinking lights of several jets move across the dark sky, hoping the bad feeling would go away, but it didn't. I had an acute moment when one of the jets seemed to hover in the sky without moving forward for at least a minute.

Then I called Lisa.

When I tried to tell her that I'd had a bad gig and reality was now a strange and terrifying spectacle for me, I began crying and making convulsive hacking sounds. She listened in silence for about twenty seconds before she said, "This is serious."

She said she was coming right over. I took the elevator down to wait for her because I was so anxious to see her and because I suspected that my existence was leaving a palpable stain on the air of my apartment that I didn't want anyone to see.

I stood in the foyer by the mailboxes, where old ladies from my building stand to wait for the bus when it rains, and by the time Lisa arrived, I was really in a state.

She wore clogs and her fuzzy pink cape, which made her look like some third-tier superhero whose defining power was a staggering capacity for empathy. She took a good look at me and said, "David, please, get in the car, OK?"

My first big mistake was getting in that car. We headed for the river, maybe to park and take an intimate stroll along and over the Charles, the footbridge, the JFK Street bridge, where I had walked solo in nighttime circles before I'd dropped out. But going through the Square, we veered right, onto Mt. Auburn Street, and ended up in the parking lot of Mt. Auburn Hospital.

"What's the big idea?" I asked.

"I want you to be safe."

"Aren't I safe with you? Or is it that you don't feel safe with me?" I chuckled and lunged at her.

She thumped the heel of her hand on my back really hard.

I looked up at her. "Why do that?"

"You're going in there," she said.

"Probably not," I said. It was dawning on me that the something that was happening to me could make Mt. Auburn Hospital into my personal roach motel. "I prefer aromatherapy," I said, trying to nuzzle her neck.

She slapped the side of my head and shouted, "Come on, stop it!"

"You really are ambivalent about me," I said. Then I started crying, which was the last thing I wanted to do.

She cried, too, and I realized how much pain I was bringing into her world.

"OK, I'll go," I said, just to show what a sane guy I was. Actually, I probably went with her because, despite everything, I loved being with her, and if she had left me by myself in that car, it would have killed me. And so was conceived mistake number two: when she opened her door and got out, I opened my door and got out.

Then I realized I'd been foolish, so I balked like a mule. She pulled on my arm. "David, if what you say is true, then they'll say the same thing and we can go home, OK?" She said hundreds of things to me that night that ended with "OK?"

"*OK*," I mimicked, though I think mimicking is evil. I felt a riff coming on. "Hey, how about that feeling you get when you see a little black bug floating in the toilet and you don't know whether it's alive or dead, and you start pissing, and your piss stirs the water and the bug starts moving and jittering and skittering on the surface of the water but you're still not sure if it's moving on its own, or if it's moving because of your piss—isn't that a strange feeling?"

"This isn't funny, David."

The rain had spread mirrors all over the parking lot. She pulled on my arm and I took a few more steps. Then I grabbed her and hugged her. She pulled away. "Stop it, David. No more!"

So I stood there. She looked me right in the eye and said, "Please come on, OK?"

"Then don't pull on my arm."

In this way, it took us fifteen minutes to cross the parking lot of Mt. Auburn Hospital, and when we got to the entrance of the emergency room, we drove the automatic door crazy, tussling half in and half out. And then I was in the hospital.

In the waiting room, the Celtics were playing the Lakers on the overhead TV, and I felt hemmed in and under surveillance.

"David, please sit down, OK?" Lisa said. It *really* embarrassed me that she said it loud enough for everyone in the waiting room to hear. She sat down, to show me how to do it. I made for the door, and she got up and blocked me and gave me this stern look in the eye. We butted stomachs. She asked the guy behind the sliding window when I was going to be seen. She was clearly tired of babysitting me. The funny thing was, when she acted sick of me, I no longer had the energy to leave the room, so the best way to keep me there was not to block my way out—because then I could bump into her!—but to just stop caring what I did.

"Sit down," she said. "Please just try. Make an effort."

"Don't patronize me," I hissed, and she said, loud enough for everyone in the waiting room to hear, "I'm not patronizing you."

"Can I have as much Zoloft as I want?" I whispered. I was trying to stay playful, to ignore the patronizing tone in her voice, but it felt as if a wire grid were pressed against my face. Talking to her made me feel as if my face were being drawn through this grid.

"You'll get as much Zoloft as you want," she said, really loud.

"What about lithium?" It was a fine-mesh grid.

Then I went for the door, and she blocked me again, so I went into my crouch, with my fists clenched and my thumbs sticking up. I flicked my thumbs under my nose, bobbing and weaving, shadow-boxing her. She dropped her arms and sighed.

The shadowboxing prompted one of the innocent bystanders in the waiting room to call out, "Hey buddy, watch the Celtics. Sit down and watch the Celtics. Give the girl a break. Sit down, right here, buddy."

I couldn't make eye contact with my buddy. He was all jeans and flannel and straight-ahead macho sense. He had a thick face and thick arms. A man like him had once decked me with a single punch during a drunken night at the Bow and Arrow.

"Don't patronize me," I said to the room.

I don't know what changed, but Lisa blocked the door even before I made a move toward it, but then the next second I did make a move toward it. When I bumped into the fuzzy pink cushion of her breasts, I felt all of my strength go out of me.

A very cheery but all-business nurse showed up. "David, would you come in here? I'd like to talk to you."

She showed me into a room that had a single examination table. There wasn't a lot of hustle and bustle, like on *ER*. She asked me whether I was on medication or seeing a doctor. She asked me if I sometimes thought of killing myself, and I told her not to patronize me. "I'm a little upset," I said, "but I'm not nuts. I'm not staying here."

"We want someone to talk to you," she said. "I'm going to get someone to talk to you, someone you'll like more than me."

Then there was some hubbub behind another door to this room, and she was called away. I saw some heads through a circle in that door, a Plexiglas portal reinforced with chicken wire. "Now I'm trusting you to wait here," she said.

As soon as she left, I went back into the waiting room. Lisa asked me what the nurse had said, and I told her, "Lisa, you should've packed a suitcase, because you're spending the night, OK? You've been placed under observation, OK?"

The nurse came back into the waiting room and said: "I told you to wait there." Then she took both Lisa and me into the triage room, and that's when Lisa totally betrayed me. She said I'd had "episodes" before. She told the nurse about my "ballistophobia," which referred to my panic attack at Out of Town News. It made me sad to realize that Lisa must have researched what had happened. She was such a good scientist. The nurse had never heard of ballistophobia, and I interrupted to explain: "Fear of death from above." It was my definition of what I now know psychology books call "an aberrant fear of projectiles." As a disorder, it belongs in a comedy routine.

They each turned to me during the instant when I spoke, then Lisa went back to the details of my "episode." When she finished, the nurse didn't ask me if this was what had actually happened, which made me very frustrated; I was afraid that from now on my own word about myself would matter less than what other people said about me. I don't wish this feeling on anyone. The nurse just looked at me, and I resisted the temptation to growl at her like a dog and instead returned her gaze blandly. I must have looked pretty convincing because Lisa evidently felt compelled to pile on evidence of my derangement. She claimed that I had tried to kill myself twice through binge drinking. This was so preposterous I had to speak up. "Can't a guy get drunk?" I asked, and the head of a curious orderly appeared behind the chicken-wire portal. I felt terrible because of how loud I had said it. Basically, I had shouted. Not having raised my voice through this whole night had been my trump card. I didn't realize how much depended on me not raising my voice until I'd raised it.

The orderly entered the room. I looked at Lisa, and she looked back, but we didn't quite make eye contact, as if we were on opposite sides of a two-way mirror and she couldn't see me from her side. Her eyes flashed down, and all of the hair on my body stood. Someone touched my elbow, and I jerked it away, setting off an escalating sequence of touches and jerks. The next thing I knew, several orderlies had me down on the floor, and I fought so hard I thought my skull would split. I wanted to stop everything, all the thrashing and struggle, by simply screaming, "I followed my bliss!" This would have sounded like more insanity to the orderlies, but it might have been the beginning of some kind of calm or even self-esteem. Yet maybe I also sensed that my career decision had been too long in coming, that I'd made too many reversals and so had weakened and broken like a piece of metal bent back and forth too many times. Up to that moment, I had assumed that everything could always be made right, that inevitably you moved on, you grew. But in the grip of those orderlies, I came to understand that the problem of being myself couldn't be solved. This made me keep thrashing like a madman, which made everything worse and brought a new and bad reality into being.

I hate to be so negative, because I know it's self-defeating and hard to listen to—which is doubly bad for me because, really, all I've ever wanted was a responsive audience—but what you don't want to see too clearly is this: You can't *know* what the right thing is. You don't even know if your own self is capable of cooperating with your deepest desires. And as a result, when you act definitively, you can actually ruin your life.